HUSH

Christian Jeremy Alecci

A friend, a hero, a witch, an angel.

This book is dedicated to Julie Baker.

If she reads this, she shall never sleep again.

I love you!

Index

Reader Beware

HUSH began as a challenge to myself. I wanted to write the most disturbing horror story I could and challenged myself on doing so. The rest of the stories in this book are scary/horror related, but the two part Hush is a story you should only read if you think you can handle it. If you want to sleep again… That being said! Happy reading! Enjoy!

Christian J. Alecci

Hush

Part 1
Early 1940s
Sussex

When I was young
We used to play
In the garden
'Cross the bay
Leaving children
All alone

In the tangles

Overgrown

He whistles

Takes us back

Never left intact

Parents, parents

Far away

Why did you ever

Let us play

To our final grave

By the bay

It just takes a day, doesn't it?

On the side of a hill right by the bay, our family's house has sat for generations. A typical Sussex stone creation. Nothing fancy. Nothing grand. Stone and cement holding tales of my ancestors back to where it began.

All alone our home sits, an island in its regard, our closest neighbors miles away. There was a particular beauty on the countryside in the early 1940s, if you enjoyed living in the gray. We were all poor because of war, but we knew enough to enjoy whatever life we could have. Blissful ignorance sang songs to me my entire youth.

A few sheep still wander the hazy hillside, but ever since the war, Mum says people will eat anything. From what I remember, my siblings and I never knew anything but happiness - my childhood was filled with laughter and good times. My pa made toys for me before he went off, and Mum spent as much time as she could making my siblings and me laugh and smile. There were such things as simple, good people. Kind people. Caring people.

My parents always did their best to keep the outside world from affecting us in our house. I used to think it was fireworks being set off in the sky. Mum made a game of it. My siblings all joined in. There always seemed to be a party. Always seemed to be an excuse for fun.

I didn't learn the word 'bomb' till I was older.

Company always was around. Mum loved guests and before Pa was sent off he seemed to enjoy social experiences as well.

But today is my special day.

Today is my seventh birthday.

Today is colored cupcakes and party favors.

Mum prepared tea and cake for the adults. She placed faded white linens on the tiny tables that sat on the dying and fading grass. Doilies were under each clay cup, most cracked or badly repaired. A few dozen adults and their children arrived for this day. My day. My birthday.

The fog was not as dense as it had been, and one was able to see a few yards ahead. That was rare. Mum used to say we lived in the clouds. Another game to play.

We all munched on meatloaf and cotton candy. We spun around in circles. We rolled down the hill. We sang the songs we knew and clapped our hands together. The adults drank sips of watered-down gin and whispered about affairs, which we had no business talking about.

A separation of taste buds are adults and children - what they like, we do not desire. Nor would any of them be rolling down the hills in their party best. So we separate, us and them. Them and us. Us. Them. We. Me.

In the chilled wind, gray make-shift paper streamers blew about, mist, as always, heavy in the air. Mum had done her best to decorate, and for the very little we had, I appreciated it with all my heart. There was no real color to our clothes. Sensible white. The dye costs too much, a luxury we cannot afford. Gray decorations on a gray day in a gray world.

A strong punch colored birthday cake amongst the gray and colorless day. My siblings woke early and made the long trek into town. They spent their pennies on frosting and strawberries for me. So through the mist and fog, the white and gray, Mum came in her party dress with the strong punch cake decorated with bright red strawberries. The only color on my birthday.

A candle was lit. An off-key song was sung. A wish was made. I couldn't tell you, or it wouldn't come true. Another party on the bay.

Now the children run off and play.

"If you get lost," Mum whispers, "just whistle, and I'll find you."

"Watch out, kiddies," Uncle Arthur jests between swigs of gin, "for the old witch in her hut near the bay. Gwen the bitch witch. She'll take your toes for her potions or maybe an eye to eat. I hear she feasts off..."

"Stop! My word," Mum gasps, "you'll give them nightmares." To me, she turns. "If you do bump into Gwendala, do not fret for she is a good... beldam. Not everything is always as it seems. Remember. Just whistle."

We hopped the stones across the bay. One, two, three. One, two, three. Off we skipped and off we ran. One, two, three. One, two, three. Into the fog. Into the gray. A garden where we all went to play.

It was well known.

Here is where the children came. Here is where they danced around. Here is where they leapt and sang. Here is where they'll be buried in the ground.

Mostly green and vine overrun. One of us always tripped. Blood was always spilled. We all began singing with latched hands. But the further we ran, the more separated we got. The further away the songs were. I was the last one to grab on and was the first one to be lost. As Mum went out of view and the party vanished in the haze, I reached out to grasp back at a fellow hand and got nothing but mist.

Our songs had been completely taken by the air.

The fog can creep on you. The haze can wrap you like a present. One second your friends are in your view, and the next they are ghostly shadows. Then just the fog. If Mum knew it would be this heavy, she would have never let us play. Out here. In the garden. By the bay. Where the children come to play.

One, two, three. One, two, three. I skip right. One, two, three. One, two, three. I skip left. I knew the minute the laughter and songs stopped, I was alone in the blanket of white. It thickened about, moist tendrils along my neck.

Wrapping me.

I let out a whistle.

Only twists of white air answer me. Echoes and shadows.

I let out a whistle.

Tentacles of fog stream around me closer.

I let out a whistle.

It is returned. Mum. There, as always, to break through the mist.

One, two, three. One, two, three. Skip left.

Another whistle.

One, two, three. One, two, three. Skip right.

Another whistle.

One, two, three. One, two, three. Skip forward.

Another whistle.

I was getting closer.

One, two, three. One, two, three. Skip…

A heavy bag came down over my head. A hard knock made contact with my skull. Strong body odor and darkness surrounded my senses. I am hoisted up into unfamiliar arms, my head loopy.

Gwendala the witch has gotten me. Fear the witch by the bay. She will take my toes for her potions, my bones to scratch her back, and that was only the beginning. Mum had smacked Uncle Arthur with his own cane when he whispered to us what Gwendala does with the genitals!

Kids have been going missing on the bay for years, and Gwendala was always blamed and then cleared. The bobbies had not found a single thing in her tiny hut.

"But she's a witch! She made them vanish!" the townsfolk said. "She's spellbinding the bobbies! She made them into ants and then crushed them! Burn her, and be done with it!"

We have a song we made up when we played:
> Gwendala will pluck your bones
> Use them to clean her teeth
> Snatch you up and turn you into an
> Apple. Ape. Apricot. Axe.
> Bean. Bird. Bear. Box.
> Car. Cup. Cake. Candle.
> Dog. Dress. Duck. Donkey.
> (And on and on and on through the rest of

the alphabet. The first one who could not continue the verse would lose to be tickled tackled by the others.)

A part of me felt I would never play these games again since Gwendala took me. But the light whistle of a strange song in my ear didn't sound like any female I had known.

Fear. It consumes the mind. An emotion that eats away anything that threatens its existence. I had forgotten about my birthday. I had forgotten about the strong punch colored cake. The doilies and the linens. The gin. The tea. Which family member was there? Which friend I had. Which present was. How many. Where. Was. Is. Broken.

My eyes began to close as the pounding in my head was all I could feel, and then I felt nothing. I only felt...

Gwendala has me on her broomstick. We are flying across the clouds and rushing toward a great battle. The sky was alive with fireworks and toy horses topped with men. Wooden guns set off great blasts or colorful ribbons. Toy soldiers fall one by one. A war is over and no one won. Gwendala laughs, and we speed off on her broom toward the candy kingdom. A place of color and smells and light. The rising peppermint turrets and deep chocolate rivers and whipped-cream clouds. Cupcake forest and licorice grass and a marshmallow dragon. "There is no war here," Gwendala sings. "Here we can eat candy till we burst."

Dream is broken. I had fallen asleep. Reality seeps in. My head pounds. The candy mountain seemed so real. An imaginary taste ran through my mouth as if I had licked the cupcake forest. I could almost taste the chocolate. But in moments of shock and fear, our mind grasps in attempts to help. Grasps. Grasps. It attempts to protect one from the truth. I am not on a broom. I am not in the candy kingdom. I am not anywhere a child should be.

"Home," he said. "I have brought you home."

But this was not my home. This was his home. I was not on a broomstick flying toward a candy kingdom. I was somewhere that shouldn't have existed. This was not the house on the hill by the bay. This man had taken me somewhere, somewhere that the energy was so dark. Goosebumps never left my skin.

A scratching. I heard it near me. Relentless scratching. Desperate scratching. Scratch. Scratch. Scratch.

Once Ma had caught a rat under a wooden box so she could go fetch Pa to kill it. I sat in front of the box as the rat desperately attempted escape. The rat's claws went as fast as they could trying to claim freedom from the wooden box. I heard a couple of them snap before Pa came and stomped it. That is what this sound is. A scratching to escape.

I soil myself the minute my nostrils open up. Have you ever smelled something for the first time and knew it was wrong? This was very wrong.

"I'm home, pets," he said. "I'm home."

The crying begins all around me. Various sexes. Various types of cries. Whimpers of fear. Tears of worry. Sobs of distress. I begin to cry, and I don't even know why.

"How did you get free?" he asked. "Hush. Looks like we get to play today. Was going to save you. Wasn't your turn. But you are not behaving. Must behave."

Immediately the scratching stopped as a child tried to scream. A hard, hollow knock sounded and then just sporadic sobs.

"Hush," he said again. "Now you've made me say it twice. Now it's time to pay a price."

The ground is wet with water and pee and dung and something else… something metallic and wet. A thick liquid substance that twists around my fingers. I remembered that metallic smell from when Mum cut her finger cooking a while back.

Blood.

"Good children stay still," he said. "Good children know better than to move."

Moving hasn't even crossed my mind. I want my mum. I want my pa. I want my cake. I want home. I want my siblings to push me. I want my hair pulled by the neighbor kid next door. I want. I want everything that I have thought was my forever and now seems gone.

I had a life. I have a life. Did I still have that life?

My wrists and ankles are tied with a metal wire. Tight.

"Good children stay still," he said lips against my ear. "Good children don't fuss. Good children stay still. Good children hush."

The rough sack remained over my head.

He keeps me in absolute darkness.

It is my only grace.

Sounds alone are enough.

"Time to play," he said. "Since you tried to scratch away, little boy, today you and I will get to play. Time to play."

The tone. The echo. The way the words flowed from his mouth. My body erupted in chills, and I couldn't help the tears.

The chill has rippled through us all. Doom has set in. Sobs abound. The chorus and medley of children. It seemed to delight him. He began to whistle again. That same strange song.

His whistling becomes more cheerful. Uppity almost. For his pets are spilling tears. For he's about to play with us.

Games I wish I never learned.

I can hear a slight struggle. But he is an adult, and we are children. The struggle didn't last. I can't see nor can I move. All the others must be bound as well. The boy must have cut his hands apart freeing them from the metal wires. All for nothing. All for…

That's when The Whistler begins his work. The sounds begin. Sounds that can never be unheard nor forgotten. How long the cries of agony went on, I am not sure. Nor am I quite sure what I was hearing. Eggs cracking. A ham being cut. Crepe paper being ripped. Fabric being scratched. Sticks being broken. A rake being brought along a rock yard. Rocks being smashed together. Metal cranks. Cogs and gadgets. Turning together.

But even at seven I know this is not what I am hearing.

I can't tune the boy's sounds out. I don't know which is worse - the boy's reverberating noises of terror or the way The Whistler whistles in joy as he does… whatever he is doing.

The Whistler takes breaks. How long can you cry for your ma and pa before you realize they are not going to come? They are never coming for him. Or for me.

"Hush. Why are you crying? I have much more work to do on you," he said. "Good children don't cry. I am making you beautiful. I am making you complete."

How long The Whistler works I do not know. But when he is done, so is the boy. Not a cry he made. Not a sound or peep. Hushed completely.

Then I heard him moving and the whistling continued. A sound I could only compare to what it sounds like when a group of people are setting up for a party. Rearranging and moving things around. Preparing a set up. Preparing. Arranging.

Then all sounds of The Whistler are gone. No more wet steps in the water. No more sounds. Just me and the other children sitting in filth and waiting.

Waiting for the games to begin again. Waiting for him to come back and play. A powerful uncertainty that splits the mind in two. Knowing nothing, expecting everything negative to occur, but not knowing when.

Time is not a friend. The concept of it is completely unknown. The woods rustle around me, and wind tickles through the rugged sack. The smells become complacent for me. I try to find comfort in concepts. Was Mum searching for me now? Was my family trying to find me? How long did they search for these missing children during war time? Would Gwendala be blamed again for crimes she obviously never committed?

I know nothing.

Here. I am nothing.

Anywhere.

I am nothing.

A boy sings in a futile attempt to comfort himself.

> O down in yonder grave, sweetheart,
> Where you and I would walk.
> The first flower that ever I saw
> Is withered to a stalk.
> The stalk is withered and dry, sweetheart,
> And the flower will never return;
> And since I lost my own sweetheart,
> What can I do but mourn?

When shall we meet again, sweetheart?
When shall we meet again?
When the oaken leaves that fall from trees
Are green and spring up again.

It comforts me. For a brief spell. A song I had heard when…

"Beautiful voice," The Whistler said, "beautiful voice." And we all begin to cry again. I did not know he was so close. I did not know he was so close. I did not know. Was he always there? Always. Just waiting and watching. Always.

"Pity," he said, "tonight will be the last time you sing."

The first sound I hear in this game I know is the boy's tongue being crudely removed. Then the eggs, cracked. The ham, sliced. The crepe paper, ripped.

This game goes on. A few times other children are brought in. I can hear them in confusion. Lost to where they are. Maybe even hoping, like I did, at first. But I have lost all my hope. No one is coming. Mum. Pa. The bobbies.

For the most part he works on the children he has already acquired. More sounds echo that I never want to put sights to. More whistling. More cracking. More grinding. More whistling. More smells.

"You are the most beautiful," he whispers into my ear, his lips brushing my skin, violating me. "You are the most incomplete. You stay hushed, for you know that this is where you're meant to be."

Once a day he pulls my head back and pours dirty water onto my face, which I gulp madly. Then he lifts the sack just enough to expose my mouth, and I am force fed tough meat. A dark laugh as I eat it. Then he pours water over my face once more, which I gulp down. Then sometimes he just pours water over my face holding the sack tight. He must enjoy the control he has over us, the power he has over our lives. He moves onto the next child and continues the routine, whistling as we gnaw on the rough meat while attempting not to choke and cough on the water that he dumps in our throats and over our faces.

I wonder what he looks like. I wonder what the face of a monster really looks like. I try to envision this man, and I see nothing but shadows, the things you fear in the night. Creatures with extended limbs and twisted faces and long claws with matching teeth.

More time passes. More moments lost. More wheels spin and moons change over.

I can tell from the crying that begins whenever he whistles, the company around me is dwindling. He also isn't bringing any new children in. A darker part of me wishes he would bring more children in. I didn't want to be whistled at. I didn't want to play.

One moment. A brave one?

I call out, "Hello?"

"Hush. It's just us now," he said. "All alone. Just us. You and me. We will play. A final game."

I had felt safe. Safe? Safer when I knew there were other children around. If you are alone, the snake will bite you. If you are in a group, your odds change.

I was the most beautiful to him. I was the most incomplete.

I cry. This delights him. He whistles.

Then I hear the sounds begin again. The cranking and grinding.

And I scream.

I let out a scream louder than I ever thought I was capable of. A sound that intensified upon itself and sent The Whistler knocked yards away. I heard it ring through the skies and echo far off. A powerful thing. An unnatural sound that calls into the forever.

"Hush! Good children don't scream!" he said. "Good children stay silent!"

With one swift move he hits my head against the stone ground, and I am out. There were no dreams. No comfort in this darkness.

It was as if my mind knew we were reaching the end and didn't even attempt to protect me from it.

I am shaken awake. Like a rag doll.

There is chaos in the air. Voices call out to each other in the woods. Emergency and importance. Action and result. Dogs bark wildly. Shots are fired into the night. It is a hunt.

A hunt for The Whistler.

I could feel myself smile in my darkness. Exaggerated hopes. They are coming for The Whistler. They are coming to take me back to my home. To my ma. To my pa. This would all be…

I feel lips pressing against my ear. Teeth biting on my ear hard enough that I bleed. He tastes my blood through the potato sack. He licks his tongue against the sack and sucks the blood through it.

"I'm the one who waits," he whispers. "I am right behind your ear. He who hides. He who is patient. I feast on your need to feel safe. Ask. When is the last time you checked that closet? The closet that is always closed. Ask yourself. The last time you looked under your bed? Don't you feel eyes on you from the corner? Coming from the slit in a door? You've been gone all day. How do you know someone didn't break into your home? When was the last time you opened that closet door? Go. Go check what's behind that door you think you were the last to close. I am the one who waits. I wait till you sleep and peer in from the window. I'm always a breath behind you. Always a second away."

Then shots were fired. Men yelled. A storm erupted around me.

He whistles right into my ear.

Calm and slow.

The same song.

Close, angry voices. Dogs surrounded me. Shots fired.

I hear The Whistler fall dead behind me. I hear his skull hit a rock and with that I hear a cracking. The Whistler is dead.

Joy filled me momentarily. I should have remained in darkness.

As the bag is lifted, I watch as the bobbies grabbed The Whistler's body to ensure he was deceased. I slowly turn my head and lose all my innocence. I didn't even see

the rescue party, the dogs, or the officers. What I see. I...
I...

We are in an old ruin. A cold, wet structure. A church at one point, perhaps. Old stone juts. Something built centuries before that had been abandoned. Age had collapsed its roof and turned it to rubble. Overrun with grass and vines and weeds.

The Whistler had set up wooden pens for us. Moved the stones about to give us each little spaces. Makeshift. Because that's not what his main focus was.

I am staring at his uncompleted masterpiece.

Most of the inside was sprayed and smeared with red. He has displayed the remains of children about. Displayed. Prepared. Arranged.

Did he consider himself an artist?

What I assumed was a boy missing most of his head was playing with the corpse of a girl. Both sets of their hands were sawed off, and their wrists were crudely sewn together. Three out of their four eyes were removed. A rod, stuck between their two chests, connected them together.

Other children were given extra body parts and limbs. A leg extended out of a girl's chest whose mouth had been removed and ears sliced off. A boy had various ears sewn onto his face, and his legs were removed and stuck to the wall behind him. He had a paper airplane in his hand as if he was going to throw it. All sewn crudely together with metal wires. He hadn't killed them before beginning this work. He had worked and toyed with each of his victims until they died during his 'play time.'

His workspace consisted of a heavy table that had straps for your feet and your hands. Next to it on a long metal roller were knives of multiple sizes, little saws, big saws, an axe that was serrated and sharpened, tools and wrenches, hammers and nails, and other weirdly shaped weapons I had never seen.

I had been next.

Me.

The worst was the torso of a beautiful little brunette that was stuck on a bicycle and suspended in the air. He had left her face intact, and the frozen look she had was of pure horror. One wheel of the bike slowly spinning, goosebumps exploded over goosebumps. He must have loved it so much he decided not to change her face. Her arms extended as if she was meant to hold someone.

Me.

I was the only one left.

It was as if someone had taken a hundred dolls and placed them all out to play. Then disfigured. Tore. Opened. Plucked. Rearranged all the pieces.

Was this what he saw the world to be?

The minute I saw the small leg on the spit roast, I began to vomit. Next to it a pile of arms and thighs and legs and hands. The strange, rough meat. He had fed us… he had fed us… us.

I blink, and I see it. In my mind. In my eye. In my eyelids. In the darkness. In my stomach. I will forever see it. Forever taste it. Forever know it. The whistle in me. Forever playing. Over and over.

A mad science experiment. A serial killer's game. A monster's play room. The pied piper's underground chambers.

All that was missing was me. Was I meant to be in the arms of the beautiful brunette girl? Or did he have another place for me?

Questions that I never need know the answers to.

It doesn't matter what his motives are... were. The reasoning behind this... macabre museum.

No. What matters is he is dead.

And what is dead may never rise.

And what is dead.

What is dead?

Part 2
Thirty Years Later
House on the Hill, Sussex

As it happens, I grew up.

As it happens, age and time took its fare.

I moved far away. Far from the horrors that happened near the house on the bay. I lived in London, attended university, and tried every drug I could. The psychedelics - the ones that made the mind spread to places it would never have discovered otherwise - were my drug of choice. But this surprised no one. Nor did anyone give me a hard time. My mind was scarred in such a way. Some things will just never go away.

As it happens, my parents aged as well. Pa, well, he never fully recovered from the war, nor from the fact he wasn't home when I was taken. Died under mysterious circumstances I could only assume were suicide. Mum lived till nearly a hundred. Their will was short and their possessions few. My siblings received knick knacks and various heirlooms.

But to me and my family, they left the house.

Many thanks.

Great joy.

I left my lover far at home and took our two children to the house on the bay. We planned to fix it up and repair what was necessary that summer. They wanted to help, and selfishly I could not fathom going alone.

Sell it off and move away. One week it would take. Just a week in the house of fog on the bay.

Humans, by nature, love to plan. Why do we continue planning when plans rarely go as we desire?

My two children. My pride and joy. Besides my lover, they are all that matter to me in life.

The first day I already questioned myself. Why did I bring them here? Why would I ever bring them here?

It had been thirty years since I was plucked away on my seventh birthday. A lot had changed here as well in their little world on the hill. Now the countryside was littered with new houses and various types of developments. Not quite the chain food restaurants and shops, but getting there.

Our house is a historical landmark, both for its age and my story. For a few years after my abduction, I did the circuit. Interviews. Talk shows. Newspapers. Radio. When I hit twenty I wrote a book, which was quickly published. It was the story of how I survived my time in The Whistler's playroom. It made me a fortune, but it didn't make anything better. It didn't make anything go away. Or sleeping any easier.

We came to flip the house and then we shall leave.

"Why are you crying?" my youths inquire. "Be happy. Smile."

And I do. For children are little blessings. I couldn't imagine how Mum felt when I was taken. I couldn't even fathom the thought.

I should never have brought them here.

I had paid to renovate the inside of my parents' house almost a decade ago when they were still alive. Not much good that did as they were too old to take care of it. Adding youth to age is quite impossible. It wasn't that that they didn't care. Nor that they didn't appreciate the gesture. But there comes a time when age wear and tear at what used to matter. Who cares if the door creaks or the pipes bark? Your legs can't hold you as long as they used to. Your back can't straighten as it once did. Let the wallpaper fade and the walls crack.

Let life fade away.

I took my parents' room.

My children, my old room.

"It's only a week," I kiss them goodnight. "It's only a week. Have no fright." My own words sounded like fables told. Lies and cheats to make the boogie man stay at bay.

It's only a week, I told myself. *Only a week. Then we shall go away.*

I close my eyes.

I fade.

Never rest. Just fade.

It began on the first night.

Was anything else expected?

During the death march hour, I sat bolt upright in bed. Drenched in sweat. My arm pointing at the door, which was shut. Just 'mares in the night. But the sounds coming from the porch were no dream, and they shivered my bones till I wanted to scream. But as a parent you aren't afforded such luxuries. One must protect; one must handle the situations.

How I moved out of the hard wool blankets and down the creaking stairs, I could not tell you. A survival instinct had taken over. In my hands, I held a plank of wood as if that would protect my children… and myself.

Then the whistle.

My bed shorts became wet. The words repeated over in my mind.

I'm the one who waits.

Another whistle.

I'm the one who waits. You are the most beautiful. The most incomplete. When's the last time you checked that closed door? How I hide and dance under the floor.

But the whistle is the wind through the trees. But the footsteps on the porch? Just creaks in the old house.

Yes. That is all. Sounds.

I still hear those sounds.

As I back away from the door, my feet drag along the floor up the stairs and back to the room my children are in. I pick them up one by one, bring them to my bedroom, and snuggle them close.

It's better if none of us are alone.

How morning came, I do not know.

My children were close and still asleep. Lost in dreams of bubble gum and Cowboys versus Indians.

Oh, the minds of babes.

The day, as days tend to go by the house of fog by the bay, was dreary.

We attempted to whitewash the house. Turn the stones from cold and gray. Bring some life to the facade, hoping a buyer would see a place they wanted their family's memories stored in.

I assumed the majority of people coming to see the house would come out of curiosity. Some horror fanatic would probably buy it. Or someone who had no idea of the horrors that lay just a league or two away.

"May we play," my children ask, "down by the bay?"

They are too young to know. Too young to have any concept or notion. Even if for some misguided moment I made the error of telling them, they wouldn't understand. When I was as young as they, I didn't even truly understand. When I was in The Whistler's playroom, I didn't understand. That took years upon years of therapy. I should have brought my therapist with me out here, but sadly, that's not a service she provides.

"No," I smile for them. "Let's play inside together."

That night the fire would not light. Yes, I put in a heater for my parents, but the children and I thought it would be nice to tell stories by the hearth. The wood was dry, the fire hot, but neither would connect. No matter what I tried or the amount of kindling I used, the fire would not start. The fireplace remained cold. The wood dry. No fire would light in this house tonight.

We sat in the spotted light and whispered of things that make us happy and content.

Jelly beans. Chocolate cake. Cookies with extra chips on them. When the sun hits the edge of the horizon and spills it's wondrous scape over the lands. Warm blankets. Kisses before bed. Sun drops on the windowsill. Soft sheets spread on the clothing line. Christmas. The crunch of fall leaves. The roasting of marshmallows on an open flame. Halloween candy. Trick or Treat.

I awoke with both children in my arms. One a toddler, and one a kid. Not much older than I was when I was taken. The purest of pure. The freshest of fresh. I would protect them.

I bring them to my parents' old room and get into bed. They wrap themselves in my arms. I know they won't be like this forever, so I cherish every moment I can get with them. While they still want to hold me close. While they still care to have me read to them before bed. When I am their best friend. Before they rebel. Before they are tarnished by the world.

We fall asleep.

A sense of peace has relaxed me.

Oh, the blessing children are.

Oh, the joy that they can bring.

During the death march hour, I sat bolt upright in bed. Drenched in sweat. My arm pointing at the door, which I knew had been shut, was slightly ajar.

From the first floor I could hear it. The whistle. The footsteps. Fear. An insidious tone. A beat in the chest.

I kissed both children for safety. I slowly climbed down the bed as not to disturb them. One, two, three. One, two, three. Footsteps on the floor leading me. One, two, three. One, two, three. Something below is waiting for me.

But the whistle is still the wind through the trees… and the footsteps on the porch… the footsteps on the porch… the footsteps on the porch… One, two, three. One, two, three.

I swing the door open.

"You came back!" a female voice snapped. "Why? What is your damage? Bah! Fool!"

On the front porch, in a tattered gown sewn with various strings and gems stood a character from my childhood. A fable. A dream. A tale. Story time was coming alive in front of my eyes. This was someone who could not have been real. But, as one would know St. Nick, I knew her.

"Gwendala?"

"Gwen," the witch spat. "Where the da-lah came from... who knows? Duh... laaaaaa."

The witch seemed younger than me, which made absolutely no sense. But does any of this? Her eyes, raccoon-dark and smudged, and her face tan from dirt and sun. Was she pretty, or was she mystical? Dreaded locks came down from her head, dark and light, crowded with gems and various colored strings and ties. Her frame small and her bosoms supple, she was a creature of the night and day. A servant of the forces and spirits. The energy radiated off her, sizzling on her skin. It was endearing. I could see how it would become an addiction.

"My parents died." I didn't know what else to say to such a fantastical creature. "I'm fixing up the house to sell it."

"Oh, I know, I know," the witch looked past me and into the house and sniffed. "Fool! You brought your offspring? I can smell them. Innocence has a stench. Babes. Youths. Untouched. Virgins. Have they spilled blood?"

"Blood?"

"Yes! Blood! An offering to the demon that haunts this land. Got to offer something to get something. A few drops on the lawn earth will do. What did you think? Just put your feet up on the deck and hope to get a tan? Go tra-la-la and all will be well?! Fool!"

I just looked at her as I would at my children when they tell me that dragons are circling the sky and mermaids are bouncing in the sea.

"Would you care to come in?"

The witch just stared back at me. Putting both hands on her knees, she squatted low and spat. She bit the side of her hand, and as the blood dripped, she smeared it across the ground in front of the door. Grabbed my neck, pulled me close, and wiped her blood on my forehead. Looking behind her for a second, the wind rustled toward the house. Leaves and dirt and stones moved in slow motion toward us.

"Ets se em. Se em... ets ne anja lucifah de me SHAAAAHANNN!!!!!" her tongue rolled in a forbidden rambling echoing only in my ears and around the house. It was a sound that traveled and covered before vanishing completely. Her dark eyes turned back to me, and she nodded plainly, "Yah. Whatever. Sure."

She twisted her way past me into the house.

"It's even uglier inside," the witch looked about displeased as if she had just bought the place, "but a piece of shit is a piece of shit. You can toss some herbs on it, and you can color it. Put a bow on it. But it's still shit."

"Can I help you?"

"Ha!" The witch let out an abrupt laugh. "You could have helped us all by not coming back. You could have prevented the end by not beginning. You could have never been born. You could have stayed in London-town in coitus and produce more babes. No. At this point, no, you can't help. You really should have died."

"Died?" I said startled. All of a sudden a rush of everything I had been through raced through my mind. "I... I survived."

"You survived." The witch was still checking the

27

house out, every nook and cranny. "That didn't send his spirit away. When a spirit has unfinished business, it will remain. Until it has taken or done what it needs. Sometimes it's a goodbye kiss. In this case, with the evil it festers, it's your life. But there is help."

"Help? I should have died? How is that helpful? What kind of help?"

The witch turned and let out a smile, her teeth as white as pearls, "You have me, you lucky dog. I've dwelled on these and other planes and with spirits before. You should never have come back, fool. But that doesn't mean this story can't have a happy ending… oh, no."

I felt an unsettling vibration as the front door shook. Then the witch fell to her knees. Her hands reached toward the space in the ceiling where the children were asleep in my parents' room, and she let out a guttural roar. Her eyes rolled into the back of her head. Above, a howling, a screeching, glass smashing apart.

I'm the one who waits.

"It's too late, Gwen," the witch called in otherworldly tones, a voice not her own. "The children. You came too late. Check the children. The children. The children. He has his bait!!"

I ran up the stairs. One, two, three. One, two, three. One, two, three. One, two, three. Where once only eight steps led the way, now a million appeared to be. One, two, three. One, two, three. One, two, three. The Whistler was taking them away from me.

I am the one who waits. I am the one who hides. I am the one who takes. I am the one who makes them cry.

I pulled open the door, a stronger force pulling it back, and then I heard them scream. My children. Echoes of my voice in theirs. Bringing me right back. For I could smell him. I could taste him. He was here.

The whistle started in my mind, then circled around the brain, and danced around in its fun and games.

I could no longer hear my children screaming. Or anything for that matter. It was in my mind. The whistle was screeching. A suction of energy. Then, as quickly as it had come, it was gone.

I knew my children were as well.

The door allowed itself to open.

The room was empty. The windows were smashed open. Sheets were thrown in every direction. Scratch marks lined the walls. No blood, but signs of struggle.

In a blind rage, I was back downstairs. My hands were around the Gwen's throat, though I knew in my gut, she had nothing to do with this.

"Why did you bring them here?" she let out. "Why did you bring them here? Fool! Fool! Nails and arms and muscles and brawn and bitch won't help this. But I can. Oh, I can."

"How?" I believed her. The energy around her was so positive and strong. "How? Tell me."

My hands were off her neck, and she was across the room somehow. In a corner pondering. Her leg raised on a chair and her hand cradling her chin. A ponderous scratch. A look to the windows and beyond.

She pointed through the open door with a long black nail. "My hut we go. The swamp. We gather what I need. Then… you know where we must go. To summon. To bring forth."

My heart stopped. "No."

The witch was next to me, "Your children are no longer on this mortal coil." She twisted a long, dirty nail around. Her words in my ear. Her breath sweet like honeysuckle. "The only hope I can see is bringing them back from the depths in which he lurks… in which… he whistles and plays."

Witchcraft. Magic. Other planes.

These are things of children's tales. But… I've seen evil. I saw evil. I experienced evil. Things like witches and goblins and ghosts seem more comprehensible to the mind than a man who takes children away from the bay and off to 'play.'

"We go," the witch nodded at me. "We go now. These are time-sensitive issues. These are rolling balls and turning tides. These are things that must be handled or lost forever."

As we left the house, I noticed that the work my children and I had done on the house today was a loss. The whitewash hadn't stuck to the house and was lying on the ground in clumps and piles, as if it had shed loose skin. No fire would be lit. No paint would hold. The cursed house from where horror stories are now told.

"Come," the witch hissed, steps ahead of me. "Much too dark out here."

Even in the night the fog held its curtain-like hold. Gwen took a step back and waved her hands around the air. "A FRAK RAR ME A DUNA!"

In a sound I could only describe as a dog being swatted in punishment, the fog retreated away. A light spilled around us. She motioned me to follow, and I did. Very close. She gave off a warmth that I could almost feel safe in, and a wave emitted from her that I could relate to my acid trip days. It took me over, and I almost forgot that my children had just been taken away by a phantasm.

As we walked down the hill of my childhood, my mind played the past. Nostalgia is a fickle thing. I could see Mum in her best dress with the strong punch cake. Doilies. Cigars. Gin. I could almost smell my birthday party that occurred on my seventh year when innocence was taken from me. The witch led the way down the hill toward the bay, but instead of crossing to the garden where we used to play, she headed another way.

"In twists and swamps upon the bay, Gwendala's den where children get lost at play," she sang in a monotone voice. "I wish I got royalties on all the songs and limericks sung about me. But all I have gotten throughout the years is blame. Blame. Blame. I have no shame. I am what I am. But a child killer? Those are darker force. Something I could never be."

The witch hopped across the rocks with a child's ease, and I found it hard to keep up with her. But the light shining about her and the energy was enough. I could have closed my eyes and sensed her the entire way. Down the hill. From the house. Near the bay.

She slowed as a blue-flamed torch came into view. She waved a hand, and it shifted to red and illuminated the entire area revealing her home. Home. House. Abode. Hut.

A small, aged-stone rumble. The roof was caving in, the windows cracked. Vines wrapped it as if attempting to squeeze it to death.

"This… is nice," I squeaked. Oh, humans. We are quiet too long and feel the need to speak. Sometimes what comes out isn't appropriate.

Gwen laughed, "Never judge what you cannot see."

She pushed the door open and led me in. The inside was clean, bigger than the house I grew up in. Carpet. Chandeliers. Fresh, upholstered furniture. Polished silver. New-looking steel fireplace. An immaculate kitchen and a table that was set. Curtains on windows that, on the inside, weren't cracked. She winked at me, and we went through a small door to the back of her house. Candles and bones. Shelves of witch's brews. Teas and leaves. Potions and lotions.

"Guaranteed to blow your mind." She tossed a potato sack my way, and I instantly dropped it. "Hold it open, fool. Supplies must be gathered. Things arranged. We are going to enter the world of the unknown and strange."

"Where did you get this?" Over my head the bag once went. Over my head and away I went. He whistled close and played his games. Over my head the bag once went. Over my head…

"A potato sack. It is a potato sack. We haven't even begun. Try to keep your mind on sanity for a while longer!" The witch was in my face, her vibrating hands on each cheek. "Stay with me. You understand? At all times.

Whether I am on this plane or another. You must stay with me."

The sack in my arms was suddenly filled with smells and herbs and candles and other shiny objects I had never seen.

Another plane.

"*We* go?" I asked. I knew there was fear dwelling in my tones. I did not intend to hide any of my emotions. Was she a protector or a trickster? She was all I had to get my children back. "*We* go?"

"Yes," wickedness danced in the shines of her dark eyes, "*we* go."

Back through the swamp. One, two, three. Jump the rocks. One, two, three. Quick across the spots. Off we go, and off we set on our way to that specific spot across the bay. Where children used to play.

One, two, three.

The fog closes in on us despite the witch's spell.

One, two, three.

My feet hit ground. Off the children go to play in the garden across the bay. The years had just caused the overgrowth to tangle upon itself. The old, stone ruins of whatever had been here at one point were all but covered. Slivers of white marble were still visible here and there, but this was now truly a garden of thorns and weeds.

The witch was holding her hand up. Slowly, she turned herself around and felt at the air. She inhaled a deep breath and looked at me, "Stop holding yours."

I exhaled. I hadn't even realized I wasn't breathing. It was as if keeping my lungs clear of this place would somehow protect me, somehow keep the memories away.

"It's this way," I pointed in the direction. In a direction I once was dragged away. When I tried to play. In the garden across the bay.

"Energy is off here," the witch lowered her hand and sniffed around. "There are not many places I wouldn't tread alone. In my many many years, I have seen many things. I helped a woman give birth to a creature that came out with a tail and hooves. I tore a malevolent spirit from a young bride who was only a teen. I un-shrunk a man's head and had to face off with the voodoo priest who sensed his spell broken. But this small patch of land in the middle of the fog… No, I'd never be here alone. It's like a whisper on your neck from a face you cannot see."

"I am happy you are here. I am grateful."

"Bah," the witch snorted as she turned to head through the makeshift path. "I don't believe in regret. But I know this is the only way to retrieve your children. And put an end to this once and for all. Children have still been going missing on these hills since you fled away. It started maybe ten years ago. Rare. Very rare. One every few years. But as we've neared to this day, more and more have been taken away."

"How?" A worthless question. But one I didn't comprehend fully, though deep down I knew the answer. It was as if he knew I was returning.

Then we were there. The ruined building covered in vines and thorns. The police had done their best to clear his playpen away. But the stones were still stained in blood. The witch's hand was on my shoulder.

"Some things are so powerful in presence that even a mortal death cannot remove them from our world. The presence doesn't always need to be evil. People can do such acts of kindness and greatness that they leave a mark. Acts of pure selflessness that an area is forever pure in white light. Some churches, maybe a playground where only children's laughter sparkled," the witch turned toward the stained stones and the place myself and so many other children were taken, "but an evil mark is much more powerful. It manifests. Out here in nowhere, especially. Without technology or interference, it grows. There is no electricity near here, no radios or signals. It can feed and grow. So many lives have been lost in this little area. So many lives taken. Death has ridden these spots with terror. You go to a battle field, and you'll get some spirits, but here... in a place where innocence was destroyed and youth was violated. That sort of evil... well... it can grow."

I couldn't move. Why did I come back? Why did I bring my children back? Why? Someone please tell me why. I could have ignored the house. I could have had a realtor take care of it. I didn't need the money. My spouse and I both worked hard and made ample due. Why did I do this?

The whistle was on my neck, and I screamed.

"The winds in the trees," the witch was holding my face and staring into my frightened eyes. "The winds in the trees. That is all that was. You want to protect yourself? Then help me. This powder must be sprinkled in a circle around this area. These candlesticks must be arranged - all seven of them - in that circle. Can you do that? I will prepare the center."

I nodded and took the potato sack.

I am the one who waits.

I placed the sack on the ground and took out a giant satchel. Inside the satchel was a deep, shiny powder of purple and blue. I began just outside the blood-stained stone area where once a spit roast sat skewering children's remains - food for us - to keep us alive so he could play.

I sprinkled the dust and made sure the circle was consistent. I didn't quite understand this all, but I understood there could be no breaks for anything to slip in. There was more than enough powder to follow the circle once, so I followed it twice.

In the center Gwen was busy arranging various objects I could not make out. I took each of the candlesticks, which seemed to be the purest of silver. No tarnishes or scratches could be found. I placed them all two steps from each other. Perfectly. Neurotically. I would do exactly as the witch commanded to a 'T.' She was the only thing protecting me. When I finished, I went to join Gwen in the center. She had a skull, a large knife, a dead bird, a naked and hairless doll, and a large white gem in the center of the circle.

She noticed me and turned to look at my work.

"Not bad for a noob," she laughed. She took my hand and, in a second, cut it with the knife and let the drops fall on the asexual doll before laying the skull and dead bird around it. She took the gem in her hands and looked up at the sky before focusing her eyes on me. "Join me."

I got down to my knees facing the witch. The skull, doll, and dead bird were between us. She took my hands and turned them, placing the gem between our palms. The gem was vibrating, and it was so cold my hand felt like it was going to freeze.

"AMAY DOMO TOUS!" she called out, and above the candlesticks, flames burst where candles would have been. "First I call the familiar."

"What is that?" Goosebumps had already exploded on my arms, and I was shivering in fear. Where are you, my children? Where are you?

"A familiar," the witch looked through me and her body was shaking slightly, though not from fear, "will protect us. If anything were to go… off."

Gwen closed her eyes and let her head fall back, her cascade of dreaded hair fanning out behind her. She hummed for a second before her lips parted and the forbidden tones began to trumpet out of her, "Ints. Te. Em. A rondume bachussa. Ets nah an. ETS NAH AN. ERCK RY MEDANYA PARAMONTIA!!!"

Her call echoed into the skies before turning in the air and flooding back down upon us. Her spell fell in raindrops about me, various words and phrases bouncing off the earth as they fell. Then fireflies were about us. Tens. Hundreds. Thousands. Millions. A sweep of tiny glows swarming about us. All in a pleasant dance. Her words faded away and gave birth to the stars. They were all spinning together into a point. Making a figure.

"What creature did you envision protecting you as a child?" The witch's eyes were on me, her voice cool. "A lion? A tiger? A bear? Speak it to no one but yourself. When you were alone and scared. What animal did you envision? What creature came to you that battled fears away?"

The Jabberwocky.

The balls of glow began to build together into a giant shape. Blurred. Until they all tightened and vanished. I panicked. The witch could feel the energy and made a noise to make it go away.

"Our familiar is here with us. It doesn't like to be seen until it is required. I brought forth the light for we are about to enter the darkest of abysses," the witch released her hands from mine leaving the gem in my hand, which was now a warm blue color, almost comforting. "Grasp it and keep it close. Never let the gem out of your hands. No matter what you see or where you go. The gem must always be with you. It will protect both of us."

"I understand."

"Then we begin."

The witch crossed her arms loosely across her chest before releasing them out to the side and up toward the skies. Stretching her dirty hands and long dark nails toward the night, she moved her shoulders about and shook her entire top half out, remaining on her knees. She closed her eyes and sat in silence for a moment. The wind whistled through the trees as if to dare her to continue on. She rolled her neck around once before beginning to mumble. The mumble grew into broken words and phrases before she was casting in a loud and terrifying way. The forbidden words, the twisted language that didn't sound right to the ear and made the brain scratch in fear.

"ITS A SHAN. ITS A SHAN. ITS A ANGE LUCIFER DE ME SHAHAN VARAGAS DE ME NASTEEEE ITS NE EIE OR ANNNN!" Gwen's hands fell to the ground as it rumbled, quaking her entire body, and her head shot up. Her eyes glossed over in white then completely blackened as if they filled with murky water.

As the world began to spin like a top, I grasped for whatever I could. Vines and thorns. The witch was sitting very still, her darkened-over eyes staring plainly at me. She began to sing. A sweet, singsong voice of a child flowed out of her mouth. A voice I once heard. Before the boy was taken to The Whistler's playpen.

Hush.

This will be the last time you will ever sing - for anyone - again.

"When will we meet again, sweetheart… When will we meet again… When the autumn leaves… that fall from trees…," her breath produced clouds of condensation, and her words twisted and turned. Multiple voices rang out from her mouth. But the last few words came in the voice I feared the most. My head began to shake in disbelief as his voice took over the air. "Are green… and spring up again. Let's play."

Gwen slammed her hands together in an explosion of darkness. I was in pitch black. I was seven again. The bag was over my head. But no. I shook my head, and I was free. My hands untied, and in my palm, the warm blue gem

39

which I was not to release, the vibration from it was as strong as could be.

From the forever a voice began. One well-known from which the children ran. He waits in shadows, he hides behind doors. He's coming for you. He's coming for us all.

"In the streets and in the waves. In the ocean and the sky that bathes. I dance with you. You dance with me. Until the day we dance to decay. 'Fear me not,' the wise man said, 'for I know all that's in your head. Here we are, my friend. You will not escape again.'"

Circus lights began to pop up along the top of a twisted hall. Pop. Pop. Pop. Pop. They ran down a forever line. The walls were studded in silver lines, and doors without handles lined the way.

"Come find me," the voice called once more before fading away.

I stared down the long hall that twisted and curved unnaturally and turned to flee. But there was nothing behind me. Even acid and shrooms had never done this. The air was heavy, and each step I took drained so much energy out of me. I trudged down the uneven hallway. In silence lingers my heart. It doesn't beat. I can't breathe. The only thing that is pushing me forward is that I can almost feel my children.

I remember my children. Their faces. Their smiles. Their purity. I can do this.

A bang behind one door sent me tumbling to the ground as the one across from it began to bang. Soon every door was shaking and knocking from behind. These weren't threatening sounds. These were sounds of escape, and from the level of the banging, it didn't take long to determine what was behind each knob-less door.

Missing children.

The doors not only had no way to open them, but there were no hinges. It was as if they were all drawn on the walls as a taunt. Tiny windows were located toward the top of each door, but they were smoked. I could see shadows moving from within. Tiny shadows.

"Behind here are my victims, and you shall never get to them no matter how hard you try. Behind here they scream. Behind here they die. Hush, I'll tell them once. Hush, I'll tell them again, but if I must remind them… they will never scream again."

His voice was in my head.

But so was another.

A familiar.

"ETS NE ENSE. ETS NE ENSE. ETS NAM AM ANT AMMMMM!!!" The witch's words pushed him away for a moment and allowed me to push forward in the hallway. For a moment, the hallway seemed to straighten. For a moment, I was almost to the door at the other end. But as I reached for the handle, as my hand grasped at the end, the room twisted upon itself. Worse than before. A roller coaster. As we twisted about and about, a voice bloomed in mind. A voice sounds in the ear. One so close to you. You can't even hear.

He begins mockingly, "ETS NE ENTS SE, eh? ETS NA SHAN. ETS NE ANS ANT AMMM. Ha. Ha. Ha."

Whispers.

Tones.

Beats.

Rhythms.

"Your witch whispers phrases that have been damned and lost to the ages. In hopes of what? Reuniting us? She succeeded. It's been so long, my pet. It's been so long, my pet. I told you. I am the one who waits. I am the one writing along the bones. You are the most beautiful. The most incomplete. You feel me along your neck. Just past where your eye can see. That space you know is there indefinitely. Do you turn to look? Do you make sure you are alone? What is comfort if not a false hope? When is the last time you checked that door? You remember closing it. But when you were gone, someone slipped in. They are in there now. Waiting for you to go to bed. Just keep reading. Just keep reading. Just keep pretending like you don't know. Someone is there. Someone is watching you. Someone is close. It's as if the air has turned rotten. Don't shiver. I will see it. I will know you know I am there. When is the last time you checked behind that closed door? For when you sleep, that's when they open. That's when they…"

The gem. The gem in my hand began to vibrate, and I felt my mind explode him out of me. I had blown a whistle that only he could hear, and it sent him writhing away. My hand, with the gem in it, began to reach forward on its own accord. The long, dark hallway that was knotted and twisted upon itself began to unravel. The door in front of me, a brush away. I push forward. The door opens. The bag is removed from my head. The music plays. A steady beat that would be appropriate if the Nazis had thrown a circus. A dark, melodic perversity.

Grays and greens have sparked this room to color. The room, a shape I could only describe as being in the center of a tree. A spider web of patterns and designs swooped upon each other, connecting the room at its top, allowing for nothing to disturb the masterpiece in the center. The Whistler's land come alive.

Children. Pieces of children.

"This is how I see them. This is my mind. Stay out of my mind. Violating me. Invading me. This is my place. This is mine!"

For the first time, a worry in his voice. I had crossed into something that was sacredly his, and he did not like it.

"Hush," I hear myself mock. "Hush."

I turned and viewed his… mind. His… sacred place.

A paper plane slowly flew in a circle around the worst art display that ever was. The beautiful brunette whose lower half had been chopped off, positioned on the bike where the seat should have been, was twitching as the wheels turned round and round. Her head slammed into the front of the bike in rage as her hands smashed against the handles. They were no longer being held out as if to hold someone… that I had always assumed was me. Her face was ice pale and her eyes a glossy blue.

A boy with half a head was spinning slowly with a girl whose face must have been run through a grater, their hands chopped off and their arms connected. A look of sullen misery on their mugs as they spun each other around. Wisps of what hair was left floated about.

Three were in a game of jump rope. The two 'holding' the rope had no appendages. The bright red rope wrapped around their necks was slowly being beat against the ground. A little boy? Maybe. The head was removed as well as the arms, and out of those holes, other legs had been placed. The body slowly spinning about as the rope circled. One foot. Then another. Then another. Then another. Then another. For all that was left, was legs.

All the children's faces were a pale I had never seen in reality. Though they spun. Though they played. Not a single one had a look of joy on their faces, and most of them had been 'touched up' by The Whistler. Most faces wouldn't have been able to smile.

My eyes fell to a small boy in a blue suit whose eyes and mouth and ears had been sewn up. He was ushering me forward with his hand. *Come join us,* I thought he would have said. *Come play with us. For now. For always.*

If I had counted right, there were one hundred and twenty-two children under puberty in this horrid, red-tangled room. Not one left intact. Not one who was left to die in peace.

The song pounded in the room. Why did I… it was the whistle. The one that shivered my bones in the night when the trees howled. As song turned to whistle it climbed in volume, it overtook the room. The children played faster. The jump rope hit the ground with purpose. The bike wheel spun at an unnatural speed. The paper airplane flew quicker. The small boy in the tattered suit ushered me forward with greater fervor.

As the whistle climbed in volume, the room began to close. The tangles of wood began to spin about each other and shut me in. Yards became inches. Inches, centimeters.

"There was always a place for you here. Always a place to rest you at bay. Your children aren't here. I had no need for them. Haven't you noticed? Nothing has changed," The Whistler's words riddled my ears, and I looked at my hands. I opened them just long enough for the gem to slip to the ground and start to become lost in the rapidly closing vines of wood.

My hands had lost their age. I didn't need a mirror to know it. I was seven again. In The Whistler's world, I would always be seven. I would always be a child. The one who was the most beautiful and incomplete. The one whose birthday was given a turn that one could never have imagined.

The grinding sounds. The breaking bones. The squishing. The clashing. The knocking. The breaking. All at once in my ears. The beautiful brunette who was just a torso reached her arms out to me. Her face still frozen in terror.

A moment. A breath. A rush of warm energy.

"The gem... the gem... the gem... ets... ne... annnnnnnnnnnnnn," Gwen's voice was in my ears. As I was propelling toward the mad circus of horrific, leftover children, I reached my hand down and grasped the gem that now burned red before it was forever lost in the wood tangles. I held my hand forward, and it connected with the sewn up face of the boy in the blue suit. At once, the gem's vibration exploded outward. They all began to melt away. The two children playing. The rope jumpers. The dancers. The singers. The card players. The bike riders. The airplane thrower. In a disgusting mush of melting souls, they disintegrated upon each other.

All that was left was me.

The red, twisted, wooden room.

I was no longer a child. I was me.

Silence was a brief break that I welcomed.

I held the gem close to me. My fear seeming to dissipate.

Then the whistle started.

A shadow in the middle of the room began to form. Slowly. Dark lines wrapped upon each other as they grew and made form.

A person's silhouette. Gwendala was coming to save me.

Oh, how the mind reaches for the pleasant when the worst is approached, but the feeling in the pit of my soul portends the horror that comes.

The silhouette was the one giving off the horrid whistle. With over-exaggerated movements, it moved one leg up and toward me and then the other. As it neared, it grew upon itself. Shadows spit over each other as feet turned into hooves and arms became longer. More fingers were sprouting from hands, morphing into claws that turned upon themselves. Horns exploded out of its massive shadow head, and a long jaw disconnected and fell down with razor-sharp teeth that rivaled each other in length. From its back, dark, jagged lines began to spider web out - tattered wings.

A monstrous giant with hooves the size of a wagon and horns gnarled into death spears approached me. It roared. From the skies, it lowered itself down to me. Its breath was rot. Its eyes were slits of horror. A creature from the end of days.

From somewhere deep, from somewhere mine, a voice came to me. It was as relaxing as wine. "This isn't real," Mum whispered to me. "This isn't real. Don't let him. Don't allow him. Break it all. Break free."

My hand reached forward on its own. Toward the ever-growing terror. Its shadow head the size of forever. Its teeth reaching into eternity.

"ADAS DE DAZ," the words flowed out of my mouth. The forbidden tongue suddenly my own. The gem had dissipated into my hand. "VARS LAS DE DONA!"

An electrified blast of white light propelled from me. The monster let out one final roar before it vanished. It looked like how I imagined a Jabberwocky as a child.

Off you go.

Off you sail.

Out of the demons.

Out of hell.

"Ets nan ense… ets eck nanste… aba shalllllllaa… varganas de me naste… ets… ne… ei… nor… ennnnnnnn."

I was back. I was sprawled on the ground. Gwen was still vibrating, but at a much less intense frequency. Her hair had bright streaks of gray through it, and her face had aged a century. Her hands were still firmly planted on the ground and had buried themselves in the earth. Small vines and insects were circling her wrists and arms. At once, her eyes went from black to glossy white to a dark, yellowish color. She exhaled and collapsed into the ground.

"Fool," she spat at me. "Take me to the swamp at once, and drop me in."

I lifted her up with what strength I could muster. A little creature she was now. Not much heavier than potato sacks.

One, two, three. One, two, three. Off to the swamp in which to dump thee.

As she fell into the water, it sparkled for a moment. Small splashes turned larger as the water bubbled. For a few minutes, the water seemed to boil at a fiery temperature. The witch slowly raised herself up onto a rock. Shook off. The gray had vanished. The wrinkles gone. Without the cakes of dirt and heavy raccoon eyes, she was a creature of beauty. Even her dress was clean of all dirt. A creature of the night and day. But a beautiful one nonetheless. She looked younger than she did when she first came to the house.

"Questions can be answered now," the witch sat on the rock and motioned for me to do the same. "That was… that was exhausting. Never has there been such an evil mind. That was no human, that was a demon."

"What happened in there?"

"Well," a long nail spun aimlessly in the air, "I am pretty sure it was a trap. I sent in the familiar to help you, but I believe it took its form for his own. You must have let that gem out of your hand, even for a second. That's the only reason that would allow that demon closer than you wanted it to be. Some windows can never be opened, and some windows can never be shut. That isn't the best of things. But you are here. I am here. I also know where your children are… I can take you to them."

"How do you know?"

"I crossed over many planes and coils while we were on the yonder. Answers can always be found. There can be a happy ending to every story. Come."

I followed her.

One, two, three. One, two, three. The fog spreads like a blanket. I wanted to flee. Gwen hummed and skipped, going so fast I almost tripped. One, two, three. One, two, three. Into the garden on the bay she was taking me.

"ERRADICKAA!!!" she howled, and from under the thick layers of vines, large wooden planks begin to spit into the air. "ASH LA REA PADUNA!" The red planks of wood dissipated in the air.

One, two, three. One, two, three.

A door appeared on the ground, and she began breaking it apart by waving her hands. Where she had blown a clearing, steps led down. A bunker built for time of war.

One, two, three. One, two, three.

The witch motioned for me to start. I gulped and began to descend. On either side of me were doors without handles. Doors with tiny, smoke-glass windows. I knew what

49

was behind the doors. I knew what was down this hall. I turned to run, but the witch motioned me forward. Her eyes far away. It felt like I was moving through quick sand. My legs were so wobbly. My heart raced. Sweat dripped down my forehead. At the end of the hallway was another door. My children were behind that door. A forever passed as I attempted to get down that hallway. An eternity moved by as my hand reached for the door.

Instinct took over.

I turned toward Gwen.

In a single motion, she flicked her hand in the air, and the red door pieces came back together darkening the entrance. She snapped her fingers in the air, and circus lights began to pop up along the top of a twisted hall. Pop. Pop. Pop. Pop. They ran down a forever line. The walls studded in silver lines and doors without handles lined the way.

Banging sounded from behind the doors.

A long groaning noise left her as her neck cracked around in different places. Her eyes weren't hers anymore. They were a pale yellow. I knew it, though I had never actually seen them. These were his eyes. They belonged to him. The Whistler.

The possessed witch slowly walked toward me as a whistle escaped her mouth. Oh, what a fool. The same tune she was humming as she led me here.

"You dropped your witch's protection gem, allowing me to enter a new host. This wouldn't be my first choice. She radiates with power, though I never cared for the company of women. But after what the humans did to my last body thirty years ago, this one will have to do." A crooked smile. Perversion in all notions spread over the witch's lips that now were not her own. Around me the whistle beat. Behind the door, my children screamed. "It's time for us to play. And with this vessel, we will have fun like never before."

The whistle picked up, and the sounds began again.

A hand waved, and my body was thrown into the room under a powerful force.

A sack fell over my head, and I was back in darkness.

The games were to begin all over again.

"Yes… it's time for us to play like never before. Which one of your children shall I begin with?"

I began to scream.

But with a clap of his hands, my mouth was sealed.

"Hush," he said, "hush. Here we can play till the worlds end and the skies fall. Here we can stay till the end of it all. Hush, I say, for screaming won't matter. Hush, I say, for you're mine forever."

One, two, three.

One, two, three.

Into eternity.

He has taken me.

Estate Sale

Arizona, 1997

"You can each pick one thing," Patricia said to her two children, "but stay in eyesight, please. Don't touch things that look breakable, and only pick an item you want. Just one. If you behave, there might be a chocolate cake at home. Understood?"

Cake, one of those magic words for children.

"Yup," both of her children said at once, bobbing their heads and smiling. But did Patricia expect them to listen, no.

Tantrums, those were expected, tantrums.

Patricia had hoped the three hours at the park would wear them out, but an ice-cream truck had rolled by, and they gave her those eyes. She knew better as a mother... but she fell for those eyes each time. The eyes that said mommy, please. On the way home from the park, they were bouncing up and down in the backseat, and out of the corner of Patricia's eye she saw the sign: Estate Sale. It was in bright blue and purple letters with stickers, a sign obviously made by a child, and underneath it were antiques, clothes, and toys.

Toys, good.

Maybe, just maybe, they would find a toy that would occupy their attention, so she could finish her work a day early. Her husband was out golfing, as norm on Sunday, and her park routine of wearing them out was disturbed by the amount of chocolate ice cream she allowed them to have.

Patricia enjoyed a routine. She finished college in four years, got her teaching degree on time, and married before she was thirty. Crystal was almost four years old, and Thomas had just turned six. Her husband, the family man, wanted more kids. They discussed him getting his balls snipped, and he went into a lecture on masculinity - so she went and got her tubes tied. No more kids. Two was enough - she could handle two.

Christopher, her husband, was angry but only for a moment. He knew having an army of four kids was ridiculous and unfair to Patricia at the end of the day. She worked long hours like he did, and asking her to take off from a job she loved wouldn't be fair. He gave her no grief but did make fun of her tied tubes, and she would snip scissors joking about his balls.

Their marriage made some other couples sick. They fought healthily, but they were the Allen family. Well behaved children and smiles on their faces, with dinner parties and many friends. Any secrets they had they told each other, and they could find agreements on almost everything. Yelling and screaming isn't the answer; conversation and calm communication is.

Patricia had parked her car on the road, as the driveway had been taken up by others searching through someone else's knick-knacks, antiques, and old toys. As her children ran off to the section where all the kid stuff was, she let her eyes wander on some antique jewelry that was cleaned and shined. Pretty pieces, real pieces - this wasn't costume jewelry but dated back maybe centuries. She went to look at a price tag on what had to be a real ruby necklace when a voice came from behind her.

"Hello." An older woman was approaching her, holding the hand of a well-dressed boy who might be around eight. The old woman's face was... old, ancient, sagging, a giant puff of white hair on her head. She was living on borrowed time, and Patricia was amazed she could move so well without a cane or any help; she even had a bit of a jump in her step. "Anything that is catching your eye?"

"Your house is beautiful," Patricia smiled. It was an old, large house that had seen a few generations. They didn't build houses like this anymore. This was more of a castle than a house, a true estate with vines wrapping the stone walls, though it didn't ramble on for thousands of square feet. It was a stone fortress of its own.

The old woman was dressed in an old but well maintained gown, and the little boy who held her hand had a bow tie on and a little suit that looked new. She had been a teacher long enough to make assumptions she knew were right; the little boy's parents had passed away, and this was his grandmother taking care of him. They probably needed every penny from this yard sale. "Such a lovely day for a yard sale."

"Most are my toys!" the little boy beamed a bright smile. "I'm too old for them. Plus granny had a few old people things that she added. My name is Thomas and I'm going to grow up to be a wizard!"

"That's enough for now, Thomas. Run off and play." The old woman smiled as Thomas picked up an older basketball and began to bounce it on the declining driveway. "Poor boy's parents died years back, and I took him in. With my husband gone now, the company is more than welcome. When I pass, he has many aunts and uncles who would be happy to take a young boy such as him in, but every cent I can get, I need. At one point, the Featherstones wore these ruby necklaces and owned fortunes, but I plan on making sure that little boy will never have to want in his life. We don't throw galas like we used to and all this expensive jewelry and furniture, it's better I put it aside for him. When I go I can't take it with me. His parents didn't have much and… I'm sorry. Most of my friends have passed away, and I don't get much adult company. A party here and there, an invitation to a fundraiser, but my days as a social belle are long gone…"

Perceptive as usual, Patricia smiled her teacher's smile she used on parent's night.

"That's ok. It seems like you have a good turnout."

The old woman's house, from what Patricia could guess, had at least six maybe seven bedrooms in its three floor estate. She assumed most of the bedrooms were for grandchildren and her other children when they visited, and now one of them held Thomas in it permanently.

"My little boy is named Billy, he just turned six." Patricia was watching her kids rummage through a gigantic box of toys. "It's a great name for a boy. When he gets a little older we'll transition into William, but he likes Billy for now. We settled on Crystal for my girl because her eyes just seemed to sparkle like them when she was born."

"Yes," the old woman said as she twitched slightly. Her face had seen many funerals and horrors, which was apparent. They say it is one thing to bury a parent, that's expected at some point in life, but to bury your children… that brings your own mortality to focus. "It means twin, the name Thomas, though my children had no idea of that when they named him. They were a young couple and never had a chance to have any other children. He's been in my care now for eight years. He was in the back seat of the car. He doesn't remember it, but I hear him crying and speaking to things at night…"

"I can't imagine a tragedy like that." Patricia had to talk to parents about all sorts of things. Why little Suzy had a bruise on her arm, or why Peter pushed every kid he came into contact with, or why Penelope kept gaining weight. There were always answers, and sadly the answers were lack of proper parenting or just misunderstandings. Suzy's dad had twisted her arm too hard when catching her off a tire swing on a playground. Peter's parents were going through a terrible divorce in which his parents kept him in the middle of, and Penelope would steal cookies and eat them in her room, a relief from the bullying she received in school and lack of care at home. Thomas' mind at such a young age wouldn't even be able to comprehend the death of his parents. If she and the old woman were friends, she would have suggested therapy. "But, bless you for taking such good care of him."

The old woman let on a smile, compassion and empathy, a slight connection.

"I have older children who have children. They live close by and come over to help out and make sure Thomas feels part of a... the family. But he's always been a strange boy. I honestly was hoping to get rid of a certain toy today, one he doesn't know I put out here. It's one thing to have imaginary friends, but... when they start demanding meals of their own or talking back to you or threatening you... they have to go. Hearing something whisper 'Make her bleed' was enough for me. I think him being separated from that doll would be for the best."

"Which toy is that?" Patricia wanted to make sure her children didn't pick it out. She had watched way too many horror films. "Please. Point it out, so I don't wind up with it."

The old woman looked at her and sighed slightly, realizing she lost her chance with Patricia to get rid of this doll. Never become too friendly with the customers, especially when you are trying to push things off on them as honesty might come out.

"Well, now you obviously won't be leaving with it. It's a giant doll, with pigtails and rosy cheeks." The old woman wrinkled her nose. "A terrible thing. It gives me the creeps just looking at it. Its eyes seemingly move with you, and it has this awful half smile between parted lips. I think it's the one who he has made an imaginary friend out of."

"Well... let's make sure... NO!"

Patricia caught out of the corner of her eye the basketball Thomas was playing with begin to roll down the long driveway moving in and out of cars on a busy road. Thomas, frustrated he lost his ball, began to run after it, and someone in a minivan who was reading a book at the wheel was pulling around the corner at an incredible speed. This was a neighborhood, a suburbia, and no one should be driving that fast to begin with.

It was all happening so fast. Patricia's adrenaline came together, and it was as if she was a varsity athlete again. She dodged down the long driveway, weaving in and out of the cars parked at the estate sale. Her feet hit the streets, and she felt it in her knees; however, her motherly instinct took over, and she threw herself at Thomas as together they went tumbling into the neighbor's grass. The ball exploded under the tire, and the woman in the minivan didn't stop driving. She saw what had happened, what she had almost did, but kept on driving faster away, not even putting the book down.

What is wrong with people?

Patricia caught the license plate and would make sure to report it.

RTS-FYA

"Are you ok?" The little boy looked at Patricia with utter fear. "It's ok. You are ok."

"Don't let grandma give her away. I saw she put her out here," was all the boy said, ignoring the fact that his life was just saved. "Please. Don't let grandma give her away. I love her."

The way the word 'love' left his lips gave her the shivers. It wasn't a child giving away a doll; it was as if it was a loved one being shipped off or his favorite dog being given away.

"I think it's best you listen to your grandma, dear." Patricia was trying to calm herself down. Her two children were at the top of the hill and had seemingly picked things from the giant toy chest and area around it. They were playing with other children that parents had brought to the estate sale, so Patricia led Thomas back to his grandmother who was standing at the edge of the driveway with both of her ancient hands on either side of her face.

"Thomas!" the old woman said loud enough that Patricia's Billy and Crystal turned. "You almost gave me a heart attack! I'm not joking… at my age you can't do things like that. Please stay up here with me. No more playing around today. Stay in my eye sight boy. My dear, you are a life saver, and I've never even gotten your name. You saved my little boy. You saved him."

All forty or so people at the yard sale were clapping as Patricia led Thomas and the old woman back up the driveway. All in the day of a teacher's work, saving one kid at a time even when she wasn't on the clock.

"I'm Patricia Allen."

"I'm Marguerite Featherstone." The old woman shook her head and waved her hands at two men who she obviously hired to help with the estate sale. Or, perhaps they were two members of her family; she couldn't tell. "No, no. I must thank you properly. Wait right here."

"Mom!" Crystal was back with her hands on her hips. "Billy won't let me have the toy I picked first. I saw it first. He saw it second. There are plenty of toys for him, but this was my toy. You said we can each pick one thing, and I picked my one thing… and…"

"Well," Patricia bent low, so she was face to face with her daughter, "go tell him I said he can pick another. I'll make sure you get the toy you wanted."

As they watched her struggle for a second, out of the back of the garage sale, two men helped Marguerite Featherstone bring forth one of the most fantastic antiques she had out. Cheaper stuff was in front, more expensive stuff in back - she should have done it the other way around, but Patricia wasn't here to tell a one hundred and something year old woman how to run her yard sale.

"This is for saving his life." Marguerite had the two guys place down a beautiful sterling silver antique mirror that was lined with crystals around the side. Decadent and elegant, it had a price tag of $2,000 on it. "You were a hero today, and a hero deserves a reward. This is the most expensive item I have here."

"This is much too decadent." Patricia knew the old woman needed every penny. "I can't accept this."

"I won't let you leave without it. It's been in my family for generations. I found it in the attic not too long ago. About a year ago while going through some old photos. Looked great in Thomas' room but, he's too young to appreciate something this valuable. But… none of that… what you did is more valuable than money." The old woman took Patricia's hands in hers, "Bless you, Patricia. My doors are open to you anytime. Seriously. If you ever need anything. Anything at all. Ever."

The old woman was hinting toward favors, and Patricia knew underneath that she meant money. Patricia would never take advantage of an old woman like that, but there were plenty of people out there that would... and probably did.

"Mommy, I want this!" Crystal had returned, thank God, without the creepy doll the woman was describing. She had an old Ken doll, and he had a football uniform on - the price tag said $50. Old woman wasn't cutting any deals. "This is what Billy took from me. This was my toy. I told him you said it was mine, so he gave it to me. He got something else."

"It's yours then deary," the old woman said as she flashed her eyes at Patricia's purse. Yes. Yes. Get the $2,000 mirror for free but $50 for the beaten up Ken doll. "What did your boy Billy pick?"

"That's a good question," Patricia said, amazed that the amount of cars had tripled since she had arrived, and the amount of people at this estate sale had filled Marguerite's yard. When a house this large is looking to sell stuff, you stop by just for curiosity sake to see what an old woman living in a mini mansion is giving away. "Billy! Get back here! It's time to get home before Daddy finishes golf. He's bringing home food, and you complain if your food is cold."

Patricia turned to the old woman.

"He actually complains if the food is hot as well. Kids at that age can be so... I can't find a pleasant enough word for it."

The old woman and Patricia shared a laugh.

"This mommy." Billy has returned with what he had picked...

Patricia almost gasped out loud, but yet again, day in and day out of a school, you learn to keep a steady face. On the inside she gasped loudly.

In her son Billy's arms was a doll the size of him, but it wasn't the one the old woman had described so vividly. It was an antique alright, something from a hundred years ago as far as Patricia was concerned.

A clown doll.

It was made of porcelain and had red hair swirled and lined all along its head. Its face painted bright white had faded but only slightly over the years; now he had more of a wan color to it as if he had a terminal illness. It was dressed in actual clown clothes, a silk white outfit with puffs of red at the arms and feet. The outfit must have been washed before the sale, for it looked brand new. Its gnarly feet were too large, and so were its hairy hands. In fact, its hands were almost twice the size that they should have been... the size of human hands. Why was their hair on its hands? Why didn't it have clown shoes on?

Its mouth was slightly ajar, and a large crack was up the side of its porcelain face. You could see the many little strings in the back that must move its mouth. Oh, please let that thing not speak. But Patricia assumed you pulled a string at the back, and it would laugh or say things kids enjoyed. The painted face had faded red circles on each side. It had been a long time since Lola had danced at the Copa.

Patricia hated its eyes the most, for it had none. Just big, round, white ovals - no eye lashes and no eyebrows. Just empty ovals.

"No."

The old woman looked shocked at Patricia's quick response.

"But Mommy!" Billy was at that age where he was likely to cause a scene. "I gave my first choice to Crystal… cause I was being nice. I was being nice. I. Was. Being. Nice. I want Mr. Chuckles."

Mr. Chuckles.

"Mommy," Crystal was at her side holding her Ken doll close, "I'm not giving up Barbie's husband. They already have vacation plans, and if they have to cancel them they will be very upset."

Which meant she was going to throw a tantrum as well.

If she said no again, it would infuse the irrational rage and terror only toddlers and young kids can release upon this world. It had been such a pleasant day, and if she came home to Christopher all distressed and the kids in a fury, his relaxing day at golf would be ruined. He wouldn't be mad, but… it had been such a nice day.

"You…," Patricia looked at the clown doll that seemed to be smiling at her, "can have Mr. Chuckles."

Crystal and Billy jumped around in a circle excited about their new toys. The simplicity of youth. Patricia went to the old woman who had a large crooked smile on her face, happy because a little girl had taken the doll that was giving her the spooks. $350 for a doll that freaks you out. When you want money, you want money.

"Oh! Fantastic!" Marguerite said as she took the money and put it in her ever growing money pouch. "Mrs. Allen. Looks like your children found what they wanted, that's $50 for Ken and $280 for the clown. That thing is almost 100 years old. Thomas never wanted it in his room, so we just kept it in the attic. But, this beautiful mirror is yours for your heroic act."

Patricia gave the woman an extra hundred dollar bill. Things were good in the financial world at home, and frankly, today had been more than she had bargained for. Good karma, right?

The two men the old woman had helping her out helped wrap the mirror in old sheets and get it in Patricia's trunk. Her kids were already in the car playing with their new dolls, a Ken doll for Barbie, and Mr. Chuckles.

Mr. Chuckles. The clown doll.

The little girl, the new owner of the creepy doll, walked down the driveway as Patricia closed the trunk of her car, and she saw that Thomas must have noticed his favorite doll being taken away.

"No!" he screamed, but it didn't sound like the voice of a child; it was much more mature. He wasn't having a temper tantrum over losing a toy. Patricia could tell. Whether it was something his parents had given to him or something very special to his heart, he loved it. That sound in his voice wasn't childish, but a mature love. "Don't take her away! Bring her back! Bring her back! She's mine!! NO!!!!"

Marguerite hushed her grandson and gave a 'just go please and quick' look down the driveway. The little girl with the creepy doll and her father got in their car. Patricia watched as Thomas stretched his fingers out.

Poor boy, Patricia thought, *Poor. Poor. Boy. Losing his parents and now having to lose his favorite doll. An imaginary friend that probably replaced his mom in his mind. He'd now have to cope with their loss like we all do when we lose something. But at such a young age... how tragic.*

On the car ride home, Billy pulled the string on the back of Mr. Chuckles. Patricia looked through her rearview mirror and watched as the mouth opened and closed, not in sync with the words.

"We are going to play games today," Mr. Chuckles let out in a slow circus clown voice. It was so old that whatever made it talk had slowed down so that the octaves were dragged much lower than they should have been. "We are going to play games forever."

Patricia shivered.

A second later, as she thought of the work she had to get done tonight, the string snapped back into place, and Mr. Chuckles let out a 'He-he-he-he-he-he-he-he-he-he-he-he."

That made her jump.

"Mr. Chuckles gets a chair." Billy was already at the dinner table before Patricia had time to set it. As if the two had had a conversation, "Just water for him, though, and a piece of bread because he knows your cooking isn't that great."

"Well how polite of Mr. Chuckles. Are you just going to sit there until dinner hun? It might be a little while."

"Yup. We are playing."

Great, this is off to a fantastic start.

"How about you and Mr. Chuckles go upstairs and play until dinner?" Billy gave her that spoiled child look, and without leaving her eye, he took the giant clown doll and slowly dragged it upstairs. "Thanks darling! Love you too!"

Children.

Patricia had gotten home from her day an hour ago, her husband probably still out with his friends after golf listening to them complain about their wives. For some reason, Patricia knew Christopher didn't complain about her; there wasn't a reason to. They talked, they never screamed at each other, and they made decisions together without overpowering the other's opinions. Having kids was something they both had agreed on, and he didn't murder her when she got her tubes tied. Between his mother's sudden death and Patricia's battle with breast cancer, they had been rocks for each other. Though their children were at those spoiled rotten ages, they were also little joys that just reminded them how beautiful life could be.

Patricia hung the beautiful mirror in her dining room. It was real silver and had the marking on the back and everything. It really was... hate to repeat a word, decadent. The waves of crystal that surrounded the silver and just how perfect of a size the oval was, you could see your entire face and torso in it. That was definitely the high point of the day.

Patricia went upstairs and silently stood at Crystal's room watching her make sure Ken and Barbie agreed on kissing before letting them kiss. It was a moment she wished she had caught with her video camera, but you can't always have those things on you. Learning manners and the rules of dating on her own, she knew if you set a good example for your children - they will follow.

When she peeked into Billy's room, he and Mr. Chuckles were whispering… to each other. Billy would pull the string at the back of the clown, and it would nod itself forward before falling backward.

"I like it here," it said in its slow and circus clown voice. Clowns talk in that cheery overly excited way to begin with, but this was slowed down so much with the aging of it that it made her shiver.

"I like it here too, Mr. Chuckles," Billy responded back. "What games shall we play?"

Billy pulled the string, and with each crank, it was pulled back into the clowns back.

"We shall play a lot of games. A lot of games. A lot of games. A lot of games."

Billy gave it a hit, and it stopped repeating itself.

"He-he-he-he-he-he," the clown let out. It took twenty seconds to get all the giggles out as she heard something inside of it roll the string all the way back together. Then, there was silence for a moment or two before the clown twitched as the string jerked from inside it.

Yup, that's enough.

That had been it for Patricia. She had checked on her children. Crystal was happy, and Billy decided to give her nightmares for the rest of her life. So, she went downstairs to finish preparing dinner. As she went out of the kitchen to set the table, Billy and Mr. Chuckles were there.

Time for Christopher to come home and buy his son one of those mini jeeps or even a Gameboy, anything to take him away from Mr. Chuckles and his not so fun loving voice. Seemingly, sensing, the garage door opened, and her husband's sports car rolled into their two-car garage.

The garage closed, and the love of her life entered through the door into the kitchen, sunburned and drunk.

"I'm drunk."

"And sunburned."

They kissed each other, and he let his tongue rub up against hers for a second. For a moment there, she let him lift her up against the wall and really kiss her. It had been close to fifteen years, but people said they still acted like newlyweds. Good. Passion needs to remain in a relationship because a healthy mixture of passion and understanding is the key to a happy marriage. Once you lose one, soon the other is lost as well.

Patricia had seen this time and time again with parents at her school through their poor kids. She would never put her children through a divorce. Never put her children through anything these other parents did. Being first a teacher and then a guidance counselor for as many years as she had been, she could write a book on what not to do. Not some cliché book on keeping sex in marriage, but a book on making sure the kids stay alright.

"Where are the monsters?" Christopher smiled, brought a hand through Patricia's hair, and rubbed the back of her head with his nails. He knew her spot. "They behave at the park, I see you have your big glass out for wine."

"Well. I brought them to a yard sale. Crystal got a Ken doll."

'A Ken doll? Cool." Christopher went to the fridge, took out a diet Coke, and began to chug it down, "Billy?"

"You can meet Mr. Chuckles on your own," Patricia shivered thinking of the deranged laugh it let out when Billy hit it. "I went to this estate sale today. You know the big house on the corner of Elmwood and Iris? That older mansion with the gorgeous rose vines in the summer? Well an old woman, Marguerite Featherstone, and her grandson live there. She took him in after his parents were killed the boy is named Thomas. He was bouncing a ball, it went rolling in the street, and my lion mother instinct must have kicked in. I dashed and caught him up before some woman in a minivan almost hit him. She didn't even have the nerve to stop herself. I caught the license plate though, RTS-FYA. I talked to the old woman for a while, and apparently, she had this yard sale to get some money to tuck away for the boy and get rid of a doll that was freaking her out. You should have seen her grandson's face when a girl took it away. He turned twenty years older in that moment; he really loved that doll. I felt bad for him. Imagine if our kids lost us. I can't imagine what... but... now that I'm done depressing you...she gave me this beautiful real silver and crystal mirror. I hung it up in the dining room because I don't think we own anything that expensive."

"What are you saying?" Christopher was up against her again, jesting. "You don't think we have a fancy house? The market is doing well, so if you want crystal, shit - I'll dangle crystal things from the bathroom flusher."

"Stop it. This is *suburban* wallpaper, my love." Patricia rubbed her nose against his, "Our house is great. A guest room with separate rooms for two kids. Not many people have a dining room, a living room, a study, a library, and an extra den for the Nintendo 64. Or... you know, your man cave. I think some would call this the American Dream. No? Unless you cheat on me, then I'll rip your balls off."

"Lorena Bobbit isn't who I married," Christopher kissed her deep again as the sound of the kitchen door opened. "I married you."

The string was pulled back, the cranking sound, the rotating of cogs and the clicking of the noisemaker.

"Let's play games."

"What the...," but Patricia slapped her hand at her husband before he could utter that last word. They had done a good job not cursing around the kids, and after little Benny Kleinert had started saying shit over and over again at school, Patricia didn't want her kids following suit. "Hey there little buddy, what do you got there?"

Christopher got down on his knees in front of his son. Crystal had gotten Patricia's auburn hair and Christopher's blue eyes. Billy had gotten Christopher's dark brown hair and Patricia's doe-like brown eyes. *Yup*, Patricia thought, *the American Dream.*

"Mr. Chuckles, this is Dad," Billy said in all seriousness. "Dad, this is Mr. Chuckles. Be nice to Mr. Chuckles, ok?"

Christopher gave Patricia a look but then turned towards his son.

"How does this sound champ?" Christopher ruffled his son's hair and pushed Mr. Chuckles out of his hands and onto the floor so he could tickle him. "Mr. Chuckles goes upstairs and in your room. You should keep him in there, ok? He can be your special friend, but don't be dragging him around. He looks fragile, and what do we say about fragile things? What happened to Mommy's expensive perfume when you played with it?"

"It broke…" Thomas put his head down. "I couldn't play video games for weeks."

"Exactly, and we all smelled like flowers for a week." Christopher negotiated successfully with his son. "We don't want Mr. Chuckles breaking cause that wouldn't be nice, and you said we have to be nice to Mr. Chuckles."

"He-He-He-He-He-He-He," the clown let out on its side as its mouth slowly opened and closed as the string fully rolled up into its back.

"Yup," Christopher got up and looked at his wife again, "bring him upstairs, ok bud?"

"Ok Dad, but he wanted to eat dinner with us. So he won't be happy later."

"Bring him upstairs." Christopher's drunk voice had turned very stern. Patricia couldn't blame him. She didn't want to eat with that thing at the table either.

Patricia watched as her son picked Mr. Chuckles up and gave them both a defeated rotten child look, which one day he would outgrow. He brought the clown out of the room and dragged it step-by-step upstairs.

"That thing?"

"They gave me the faces, Christopher."

"Ohhhh," Christopher said dramatically falling to his knees and crawling toward his wife, "the faces. How we fall mercy to the faces."

He wrapped his arms around his wife's legs and looked up doing his best impression of a begging child.

"When's dinner?"

"Remind me why I married you?" Patricia slapped him with a kitchen towel. "I might as well have bought myself a non-skip cd player with the amount of money I spent today on those kids. I hope these golf days are worth it."

"With guns like these," Christopher was on his feet and flexing, "that's where you close all the big business deals. The market is up Patricia, and soon we can start traveling to Europe. I thought I'd bring you wherever you wanted next year. Maybe... that's why you married me? For stuff like that?"

"Nah," Patricia went back to cutting the chicken up, "it's definitely the guns."

That night Christopher was awoken by a giggle he heard downstairs.

The clock read 3:15.

His wife had heard it too, and before Christopher said he would check it out, in a monotone voice she let out, "Mr. Chuckles."

"See," he whispered into her ear and kissed it as he slowly climbed out of bed, "it wasn't creepy until you made it creepy."

Christopher kept a metal bat behind his door in case of an actual break in or intruder. He didn't know why, but he picked it up. Each floorboard he stepped on as he neared the stairs that led to downstairs creaked just slightly, which he had never fully heard before. He climbed down each step slowly and noticed that the tv in the game room was on, but it was all fuzz.

It didn't seem like anyone was in there. He heard thumping in the kitchen and a rattling at a drawer.

"Whoever is in there," Christopher dropped his voice to sound as much like a tough cop as he could, which he nailed pretty perfectly, "I am armed."

With his foot, he kicked the swinging door to the kitchen open. He slowly made his way in, the bat ready to swing at anything.

All the drawers and all the cabinets had been opened. Set on the table was a plate with half-eaten food and spilt milk. Whomever had made themselves a midnight snack had fled as they heard Christopher approaching.

'He-He-He-He-He-He-He-He-He-He."

The terrible slow laughter of a once happy clown. A creepy reminder of when something was new and has now gone old. In the silence of the house, he could hear the winding of the string, the turning of the cogs, and the cracking of the toy as its appendages moved. It came from under the kitchen table, and Christopher tried to keep his composure.

He froze. Behind him, the kitchen door opened and swung back and forth. Back and forth. Christopher looked under the table as the kitchen door was swinging back and forth. Back and forth. He saw the tiny feet scurry, and for a second, he heard his wife's voice.

Mr. Chuckles.

He couldn't move for a second as he had never experienced this level of fear before. He could understand a human breaking in, but this... this was supernatural. As the door stopped swinging, he pushed it open with the bat. Slowly and silently stepping through the dining room, he caught a reflection of himself in the new mirror his wife had received. Wow, a day in the sun had done him well - he looked good. Like years had been taken from him. Vanity.

But inside he was terrified, and from the mirror's reflection, he saw the tv go from fuzz to Mario Kart. He quickly turned, bat ready.

"Billy. If that's you, you will be getting in big trouble little buddy," Christopher grumbled under his breath - if he was a little kid he would of peed himself by now - "for scaring the holy shit out of daddy."

He entered the den where he had set up a make-shift man cave for him and his son. It was filled with the newest games for the Nintendo 64, Dreamcast, and Sega. He was as much of a game dork as his son was. He probably spent more time in there than they did.

A moment ago, Peach had swerved and was bouncing into a wall on Rainbow Road. Who picks Rainbow Road anyway? That's torture enough in itself. There was no one in the game room, so he switched both the tv and Nintendo 64 off.

The kitchen door swung open and closed again. Christopher heard it, along with the scurrying of feet. A chair at the dining room table scratched the wood floor as it was pulled back, like nails on the chalkboard. The sound of a string being pulled all the way back. Cog by cog, inch by inch, it twisted back.

"This is a happy home. One filled with love where no one gets left alone," Mr. Chuckles very slowly said, so slowly as Christopher stared at it sitting on the dining room table. Facing him, its white orbed eyes just stared blankly back at him. The string inside clicked, and the clown's head fell loosely to one side. It was smiling at him. "Games we will play. Games we will love. Together forever we shall dance the dance of dance of dance of dance of dance of dance…"

Christopher stood there, bat ready. Breathing heavily in and out, he could feel his heart palpitating. He went to sigh as the final part of the string wrapped, and he heard, "He-He-He-He-He-He-He-He-He-He-He-He."

Yup, Christopher thought, sorry Billy but this thing is going to wind up in the trash.

Christopher went into the kitchen, eyes on the giant clown doll the entire time, and then to the garage to get a garbage bag. Christopher was going to swing Mr. Chuckles against the ground outside a few times and leave it out for trash. To hell with that clown doll.

But, when Christopher returned to the dining room, Mr. Chuckles was gone. Christopher had always been sensitive to energies; it might be why he did so well in the financial wealth management world. He could tell when a client was about to say yes or no and even when his wife was going to be in a bad mood, so he could get her flowers and cheer her up. The energy in the dining room was so uncomfortable that he was frozen in place for a second.

"It's just a toy," Christopher said reassuring himself. "It's just a toy."

At that moment from his daughter's room, he heard screaming. Christopher gripped the bat and flew up the stairs. His wife was down the hallway before he could make it, and when he opened the door...

Mr. Chuckles was sitting next to their daughter's head, its hairy hand on her forehead just sitting there. It's other hand was near her neck, it's nails to close comfort.

"It told me we should play games," Crystal was crying as she got out of bed and wrapped one arm around her mom and dad's leg. "It told me it had rules for its games."

Billy was at the door wiping his eyes, just waking up. "What's up?"

"Nothing," Patricia kissed him on his forehead, "go back to bed."

"Mr. Chuckles!" Billy went over and wrapped the doll in his arms. "Crystal this is my toy! You got your toy today! Thief! Mr. Chuckles, come back to bed with me. My sister doesn't want to play your games, but I do."

As Billy passed by his parents and went back into his room, the final cog twisted, and the clown let out a louder, "He-he-he-he-he-he-he-he-he-he-he-he."

Christopher and Patricia both had the same look of horror on their faces.

"That sounds to me like some demon shit." Rhonda stuck her fork into her salad, "Mr. Jangles is going to Amityville ya'll."

Patricia was in the teacher's lounge for lunch break. Her best friend, through pure luck, was Rhonda, the principal. Patricia had never sucked up to anyone in her life - Rhonda hated suck ups. They had connected instantly through honesty, the best way to connect with anyone.

Patricia wasn't hungry. "Rhonda, I tried to take the toy... that thing away from Billy this morning. Yah know to bring it to a field and burn it or put it in a trash disposal, but he gave me the eyes. Don't your kids give you 'the eyes?' Not the 'please we want ice cream eyes' but the 'if you take this from me I'll throw a temper tantrum that you'll regret' eyes?"

"You bet they do." Out of the corner of her eye she caught Ms. Frankel. "Betsy! We all appreciate you lost the amount of weight you did, but go home and change. You are dressed like one of the girls on the cheerleading squad I yell at, almost daily. Go home. Go home. I'm sorry, Patricia. Yes, the eyes, but mine are fifteen and thirteen. By then the eyes are trouble. You don't give into them as easily as you do when they are younger. No offense. I'm guilty as well. When my little brats were your kids' ages, I couldn't say no either, but you learn to toughen up and learn to realize what they want isn't always what they need. Did Billy really need Pennywise?"

"Well…" Patricia sat back. Rhonda had brought up *IT*, a terrifying story about a clown. She was now running over every Stephen King book she had read and every horror film she had seen. "What am I supposed to do with Mr. Chuckles? Get it an exorcism? Burn it in flames? Call in a priest?"

"My cousin Chanel has this cousin Rachael who knows this girl," Rhonda sat back obviously not taking this as a joke at all. Folding her big, black arms across her chest, she was dressed as always in a St. John business woman's outfit. Fashionable yet set the air in the school, she was here for business, and if any kid's UFO pants fell below their buttocks, she had belts in her office of various sizes to make sure they stayed up. "Oh hunny, when I first moved into town we lived in an old house. One where my hubby had fixed up all the pipes and plumbing, and the floorboards never squeaked when I walked on them. But at nighttime, I heard the scratching across the floor. Furniture would move on it's own, and a rocking chair in the living room would just rock back and forth, back and forth… Well Rachael's knew that girl I was just talking about. Julia Baker, her name was, she has to be eighteen-year-old now, a red head witch or something. She came by, we spent a night in a hotel, and we came home. You could just feel whatever was there was gone. No more scratching. No more whispering. No more sinister rocking chair. This redheaded girl did her work well."

"So, after that your toys stopped moving? The scratching stopped? It was all over?" Rhonda nodded her head, and Patricia let hers fall into her hands shaking her head. "I feel like I'm going crazy. You see the books I read, and you know the movies we go watch together. The first night is always just warnings. The second night someone gets hurt. The third night… well from there on out you are - forgive my French - le fucked."

"You aren't crazy. The people who think there aren't things that go bump in the night are. We are teachers at a school. How about the stuff we see here every day? Some of the things the kids tell me in the privacy of my office give me shivers. At their ages, they are much more susceptible to these types of things. You call Ms. Julia Baker, and you tell her Rhonda said to get her skinny white ass over to your house. Tonight."

"Tonight?" Patricia was supposed to have the Henderson family over for dinner. However, in her mind she heard the clown doll laughing that long drawn out he-

he-he-he-he-he-he-he. Now she could also imagine, with the size of that thing's hands, how easily it could grapple a knife. "Yup. Give me that number, and I'll call her."

"You make sure you tell her that Rhonda said tonight. You mention my name, and that girl will jump because she owes me a favor or two. Tell her it's down to one favor. You be sure of that."

Patricia reached her hand over to Rhonda and wrapped it in hers, but Rhonda retracted.

"I'm supposed to be the hard iron principal of our fair school. Give me a hug later in my office or something because - Coach Caldwell! I heard you let Missy Taylor cut gym class because she didn't want to get her hair all sweaty. I hate to have to tell you how to do your job, but now, now let me tell you how to do your job."

Rhonda was across the teacher's lounge, doing her work, an example for all. She was one of the best principals Patricia had ever seen, and she had worked in a few different school districts over the years until she landed this job first as a teacher then a guidance counselor at a nice school in a great neighborhood run by a principal who had empathy and compassion, hidden under iron and fear. There were no fights in the hallway, and they had the highest graduation rate among the highest GPAs in the surrounding communities.

But what did that matter right now? If Patricia couldn't get rid of Mr. Chuckles, she might not be here to see the school grow even more.

In front of her was Julia Baker's card, a black card with her name in crimson on the front and just a number on the back. Rhonda was a good judge of character, but Patricia hoped she wasn't inviting some loon into her house. Either way, she wasn't going to chance that Mr. Chuckles had games that would get worse as the nights progressed.

Julia Baker was kicking the dirt off the bottom of her heel as she stood on the sidewalk in front of the Allen house.

Julia was dressed in a simple black and elegant dress, something you would wear to a funeral, falling down to above her heels. Her red hair fell in loose curls around her, her face pale and speckled with freckles, and her blue eyes inquisitive.

Taking a moment, she walked around the house, as she knew no one would notice her, so she took her time. She ran her eyes and hand through the air, catching the energy, but from what both Rhonda and Patricia told her on the phone, this wasn't… this was different.

The air. The energy. The feeling.

Julia returned to the front porch, reached a black painted nail, and rang the doorbell. It was one of those doorbells that wasn't just a chime but a little song, one she had heard church bells sing. Moments later, a tall handsome man answered the door.

"Hello," Christopher said with a little worry in his eyes. It had taken Patricia an hour to convince him that this was a good idea because deep down, he knew he wasn't imagining things last night. Mr. Chuckles had been bouncing around downstairs, and he wasn't about to have a repeat of it. Its large hands on his little daughter's head... With those hands it could... He had a feeling a metal bat was no use. "You must be..."

"Julia Baker." Her smile was sweet, and Christopher relaxed into it, "Christopher Allen?"

"Yes. Yes. Come in. Come in."

As Julia stepped into the house, she held up her hand slightly. A hand went to the necklace around her neck, as she slowly stepped around, her hand slowly moving through the air. Patricia was at the den cleaning down the kid's table and watched her from there. Julia was a beautiful young lady with natural red hair and eyes that darted all over the place as she slowly moved her hand about. First from the floor to the ceiling to the upstairs to where the kids' rooms should be.

This is nothing like Rhonda's house, Julia thought. *This is nothing like anything I've experienced before.*

Her hand, as if on its own, flew around towards the dining room. A young boy, maybe six, sat at a chair next to the head of the table. At the head of the table was a clown doll, if you could call it that, one of those antiques that at some point people would consider valuable. Time and lack of care had turned it into something atrocious.

Julia's hand fell as she found the source of energy: the dining room.

"Hello there," Julia walked past Patricia giving her a small smile. She could feel the presence of a child upstairs. "What's your name?"

"I'm Billy," the boy said with spoiled attitude in his voice. "Mr. Chuckles would like it if you left."

Billy pulled the string at the back of the doll, which caused the doll's head to swing back and forth. The long wide scar on the side of its cheek showed the strings where the mouth moved up and down, and it tilted its head to one side. The string began to roll back into the doll, and the voice that came out of it gave everyone shivers.

"Games will be played," Mr. Chuckles slowed voice began to rattle off. "Come play them now and again and again and again and again."

"Mrs. Allen?" Julia turned and kept the pleasant smile on her face. If she could keep the smile on her face when faced up against a demon, she could keep it on for Mr. Chuckles. "I normally ask the family to leave for the night, but... this is... Is there a child upstairs?"

Patricia looked her over. She was after all a stranger in her house, but Rhonda had never led her wrong. Rhonda had seen how well she did as a teacher, guiding young students, and instantly promoted her to a guidance counselor after firing the other guidance counselor who had been confiscating pot and other drugs just to bring home to use for himself. That was a day when Rhonda herself brought in the nurse to drug test him. If she trusted this woman, so would Patricia.

"My daughter Crystal, woke up screaming last night. Mr... the doll... it was sitting in her room. Hand on her head... other one was near her throat..."

The string snapped back into place even slower than before, and Mr. Chuckles let out a "He-he-he-he-he-he-he-he-he-he-he."

All three adults looked at the doll whose head tilted to the other side when it was done laughing. Julia held her hand up slowly. The energy was definitely coming from the dining room, but something… it was an odd feeling… told her, she needed the entire family in the dining room, not to be alone in the house overnight. In her profession, it was her gut instinct she went with at all times.

Listen to your gut, her aunt had always said. *Always listen to your gut, fool.*

"Keep your daughter Crystal upstairs. If you may, Rhonda gave me her version of what happened last night, but the game of telephone is always thrown off course. If you don't mind Mr. and Mrs. Allen, please, in your own words tell me what happened from when you got the… doll… to what happened last night… to anything else. The more information I know, the more it can help."

They all sat at the dining room table. Julia allowed the Allen family to pick the seats in which they wanted to sit and left her the head of the table. She had predicted that none of them wanted to be face to face with Mr. Chuckles.

Patricia had explained the old woman and the yard sale, the little boy named Thomas who she had saved, the mirror the woman gave to her, and the Ken doll Billy had wanted and how he had settled on Mr. Chuckles. Then Christopher talked about what happened the night before with the video games being on, the sounds in the dining

84

room, and the feet scurrying around. Yes, from everything they were saying, the clown doll needed an exorcism.

But…

"When I came home from work today," Patricia put her hand on her husband Christopher's, "he was upstairs showering, and when he came down… you tell her, dear."

"Billy was just sitting in the dining room. Talking to Mr. Chuckles. Whispering. I could swear I heard a voice answering him. It was as if I interrupted their conversation."

"I'm here," Billy said with even more attitude. "Don't talk about me like I'm not. I'm here."

"Billy," Julia smiled at him, and he flinched slightly, "do you and Mr. Chuckles talk?"

"I'm not supposed to tell."

"What does that mean, buddy?" Christopher went to ruffle his son's hair, but his son flinched away. "Billy?"

"I. Am. Not. Supposed. To. Tell." Billy sat back, but not before pulling the string on the clown doll. It lurched forward towards that table and then back to the chair, its head tilting to the sides. Through the cut in its cheek, you could see the strings move like seeing inside someone's mouth as they talked. As the string rolled back in, even slower and less clown like, the doll let out, "The games have begun."

"Are you sure you don't want us to leave for the night?" Patricia quickly looked over at Julia and then her husband. "We can all rent a hotel room, somewhere nice, and spa and relax and even maybe get a suite and…"

"No," Julia didn't know why quite yet, but they weren't to leave the house. "Nothing. Nothing changes. Patricia, I'm sorry, but can I bother you for some tea."

"Some sort of witch stuff?" Patricia asked in a friendly voice as she went to the kitchen.

"No, I just like tea."

"Forgive my wife," Christopher said smiling over at Julia, "she's just stressed."

"For what?" Julia missed whatever she needed to be forgiven for.

"Calling you a witch."

"Oh," Julia laughed and millions of thoughts ran through her head. "Trust me. I've been called a lot worse throughout my few years of doing this, but I continue to do this, so families like you can sleep better at night. As much as I'm helping you, you are helping me. This is an ever-learning profession. There is no master degree in this line of work. You need to search out priests who have performed exorcisms and find the right women down in New Orleans who have actually seen voodoo firsthand or a nun who watched the crosses in her room all slowly get turned around while her bed flew to the ceiling. My aunt has been a huge help as she's a witch herself. She stopped this breeding ground of demons, hundreds of women taken and seeded with demons that would be... Sorry."

Billy was staring at Julia with wide eyes. She was scaring the child. How was she scaring the child? Even at six, if a clown doll began talking to her, it would break that wall - the wall between what we believe is out there and what is actually out there. The unexpected would seem expected, and the unknown would be opened up. Imagination would grow and wonder. Nothing she had said was anything worse than an awful antique clown doll talking and moving around.

Listen to your gut, fool. Her aunt's voice was in her head. *Don't be a fool. Spirits, demons, conjurers, the smart ones fool you.*

"Billy," Julia leaned forward on her arms and smiled kindly at the child, "what does Mr. Chuckles say to you?"

Billy looked right back at Julia, a real brat for his age, and pulled the string all the way back until a popping sound was heard. It was the furthest the string could be pulled. As it slowly wrapped around the wood inside of it, the clown let out, "The games have begun, and the drum goes boom." Mr. Chuckle's head tilted as the string rolled back into it, causing it to almost cough. But as the final part of the string smacked back into place, both of Mr. Chuckles' hands fell forward onto the table, hairy hands way too large and inappropriate for a doll, and as slowly as possible. Each sound worse than the last was let out, "He-he-he-he-he-he-he-he-he-he-he-he-he-he-he-he-he-he-he-he-he-he-he-he-he-he-he."

"Candles. Chalk circle with symbols. Feathers. Bones. A skull." Patricia said, "This is a horror movie. Tell me we each need to drop blood."

"You do." Julia was no longer smiling, but instead she was focusing on the cup her aunt had given to her.

Various gifts sent to Julia over the year always seemed to help her in her line of work. The cup had many faces on it, and they all were in great agony. Tiny char faces with jaws ajar or contorted. "A devil's cup to summon forth the demon from within that doll."

As Julia went around and pricked each member of the Allen family, besides Crystal because in her gut the little girl was to remain upstairs, she caught her reflection in the mirror on the dining room wall. Just hitting twenty, she was a beauty with her long red hair, her perfect sparkle of freckles, her eyes that glittered and glowed… Had she lost some weight? Was her skin tanner?

"Ouch," Billy predictably said as she pricked his finger, "you are a witch!"

"Maybe I am. I prefer medium, psychic…" Julia knew the six year old didn't know what she was saying. She kissed his finger, and he smiled. "I'm here to help you. I'm here to help your whole family before something happens to all of them. You wouldn't want that would you?"

For a second, he looked up to where his little sister's room was and gave a spoiled look. Julia laid a hand on the skin of his shoulder; the attitude subsided, and he smiled again.

"I love them."

"Ets ne en. Ets ne en. Ets ne anja lucifah de schamalaze." Julia began to rumble as they all held hands. The words spread around the circle tightening it, not leaving the room or moving. Whispers of her callings, echoes, and flutters of words echoed throughout the room. They weren't just words; they were calls to action.

Mr. Chuckles was in the middle of the chalk circle, the family's blood dripping down the skull with feathers sticking out of its eyes. The rest of the family's blood had been poured over the clown who was lying face up towards the modest chandelier they had in their dining room.

Julia's eyes flashed everywhere. From Patricia, to the chandelier, to Christopher, to the mirror, to Billy, and then to Mr. Chuckles. Exhaling heavily, she concentrated on the energy in the room, all of the energy, and inhaled as much as she could. She inhaled both good and bad, but nothing bad came from the Allen family, which let Julia smile. It was very rare you met a family that was just happy.

Then she felt the door open. That invisible door that only certain powers can open and shut. That door that could cause chaos and rupture reality or send a demonic being back from which it came. Julia saw it. Outlined in horror with long skinny hands reaching out from it, it was plastered on the corner of the ceiling reaching down towards Mr. Chuckles.

We are friends here, Julia thought towards the thin black murky dripping arms that were reaching down towards everyone and everything. *But the doll must go.*

"Anje numas de me tala. Anje numas de me tala. Anje numas de me tala. A lora. A lora. A don media…"

The table began to shake.

The long arms from the ceiling began to focus their reach on Mr. Chuckles. Julia needed to send it back to

89

where it came from, and they had come to ensure it traveled smoothly. One wrong word, one wrong phrase, and the hands would grab the wrong person and drag them through… what Julia only assumed was hell.

"Meda circe. Meda circe. Anvas und malasha. Anvas malasha…"

The lights of the chandelier in the dining room began to fluctuate from a darkness deep to a light so strong. It blinded. It blinded so much that Billy broke the circle to cover his eyes.

"Billy!" Julia screamed as she felt the energy and her words begin to dissipate, the hands on the corner of the wall turning their grasp toward the six year old. "Join hands! Join hands!"

Billy quickly rejoined hands, and as he did, the otherworldly hands went back to grasping out towards Mr. Chuckles.

"Lucifah de fallante! Fallante friejndas dont de me und SCHLAZA!"

The lights exploded into the mirror on the wall, which shot out a direct light at Mr. Chuckles. He began to laugh in deeper tones than his strings ever allowed him to. One large hairy hand at a time, it brought itself up to its full height in its silk clown suit with the red ruffles at the end. The oversized feet that were scratched and scarred with age. The swirly swigs of red hair on top of his face. His mouth began to move around as if to strengthen the muscles in it again. His white orbs of eyes were glowing from the bursts of light coming from the mirror. Blood was dripping down his face and down his mouth - the blood of the Allen family.

It held a hand out to the door that Julia opened, the door to the other side, the door that would take the demon inside this doll and bring it back from which it came. It slammed shut, and Julia felt like she had been slapped across the face.

One of the only spells she knew had been broken. She had sent dozens of creatures back through that door, the hands always wrapping the force in their grasp and bringing them back. It had never been broken before. Not by a skin-wraith, not by a banshee, but Mr. Chuckles shut the door with a flick of his huge oversized hands.

"Hello Billy." Mr. Chuckles' head cracked, and the strings in its mouth moved up and down as it slowly spun it's head completely around and then turned its body towards the little boy. It was stretching its hands in and out and spun its head around to Julia as if to taunt her. "Let's play our first game, shall we?"

Billy was white with fear and couldn't move. Mr. Chuckles took a few steps down the dining room table towards him, the glow of light from the mirror still upon him. He cracked each knuckle on his large hands.

"I call it strangle." Mr. Chuckles' deep raspy voice had a smoker's laugh to it as he bent low to wrap his large hairy hands around Billy's neck. Billy was crying and wetting himself as the doll reached out towards him. "Strangle. Strangle. Strangle. He-he-he-he-he-he-he-he-he-he-he."

"ANJA DUN DE EST ENZE ANVAS MALASHA DE ME CON!" cried Julia as the doll wrapped its hands around Billy's' neck. "ESTE NE EN ESTE NE EN ANJA LUCIFAH FRANJAIAS SUMMONITH…"

Christopher broke the circle, and all the energy rushed right back into Julia sending her flying against the wall. Christopher lifted the doll who attempted to wrap its hands around his neck, but Christopher stood over six feet and was an athlete.

Mr. Chuckles was taken by the legs and swung into the mirror, once causing a spider web to crawl across the surface. Then he reeled the doll back as much as he could and brought it around smashing it and directing it into the mirror, causing its head to explode and the mirror to smash and fall to the floor.

Mr. Chuckles lay broken on the floor, not moving and not talking. Christopher stomped on its body causing it to crack, and then he ripped the string off its back. He dragged the doll into the kitchen, ruffled through drawers, and kicked the door open to the backyard.

"He's going to burn it, Patricia."

"How do you know?"

"I just do." Julia looked over at Billy who was shaking in his seat, staring down at the broken mirror. He was crying. "Patricia, go make sure your husband doesn't cause a larger fire."

"He's normally good with these… oh you… saw… you, mean."

"Yes," Julia nodded. She had seen it. Making her

way over to Billy, she kneeled down next to him. "Why are you crying? I'm sorry about your toy."

"My sister has my toy. All I wanted was that Ken doll." Billy looked angrily up at where his sister was probably either asleep or playing with Barbies. But Julia knew she was sound asleep dreaming of unicorns. She was riding one through a meadow of sunflowers.

Yes, it was a good idea to keep her upstairs during this.

"What about Mr. Chuckles?"

Julia placed a hand on his shoulder and lifted his head with her finger.

Meet my eyes, and tell me the truth boy.

"I snuck out of my room last night to play video games and have a snack," Billy admitted. "Took that ugly doll with me and almost got caught by my dad. I left it in Crystal's room to scare her this morning."

"When your mom came home from work, though, she said you were talking to someone. Who were you talking to?"

"Her." Billy looked at the shards of the mirror. "She told me not to talk about her. She told me to break the mirror. But… she scared me. She wanted my blood."

Patricia looked at the antique mirror that lay on the floor. Looked at the perfect shards that had fallen off of it after it had broken. They were perfect in the sense that none of them would cause you to bleed. Julia picked a large piece of one up and slipped it into her pocket. She didn't know why, but she felt like she needed it.

Her?

"Well." Patricia was at the front door, and Mr. Chuckles' burnt remains were in a trash bag in Julia's hands. She had insisted they could just get rid of it themselves, but the Allen's were dead-set on sending Julia with a parting gift. "Rhonda has never led me wrong. She says she owes you less of a favor now. I just didn't think you'd be so young. How old are you? Eighteen?"

"I just turned twenty. Believe it or not, I've been doing this since I was sixteen. You could say it runs in the family. Rhonda has quite the sense of humor. She actually owes me three favors now. That's her cute way of putting it. I've saved her a couple of times now. Her son as well. Tell her to add another tick to her bedpost. I'll come collecting one of these days."

"See, that sounded witchy," Patricia joked, and Julia smiled, though these witch jokes were getting annoying.

"Can you stop calling her a witch?" Christopher looked at his wife, "Is her nose green? Does she fly on a broomstick?"

"Mr. Allen, my broomstick is actually parked down the block," Julia laughed with him as she appreciated the support. "It's ok. Most don't know what to make of me to begin with. You hear witch, and you think of some awful person who does awful things for selfish reasons. I'm technically a medium, but I'm always around to help."

"Are there…" Patricia obviously felt bad as she didn't realize she had been referring to Julia as a witch all night. Julia sensed genuine regret on this matter, so she continued to smile. "Are there... wicked witches out there?"

"Not everyone walks in the light, Mrs. Allen. Some prefer the dark. I've never encountered one... and I hope not to. There is only so much brightness one can bring forth, but darkness can encompass everything."

"Is there anything we can do for you? Pay you?" Christopher had his arm around his wife. "It seems like you really saved our lives in there. I hate to leave you with just that thing in a trash bag. You saved our family."

"I disagree. It seems like you have some muscle in you and know how to crush and burn a demon." Julia smiled, though the words didn't seem right. This wasn't a demon. Mr. Chuckles was a doll that a little spoiled boy used to spook his family, but what had made the clown doll stand up? What had made his hairy hands wrap around Billy's neck. *Damnit*, Julia thought, *why can't I just leave this alone.* "Hey. Where exactly did you say this estate sale was? I want to stop by and make sure that old woman, Mrs. Featherstone, doesn't have any other haunted objects to worry about."

Patricia gave her the address. They bid their farewells. Patricia actually gave Julia a huge hug, which she allowed, though she didn't feel like she deserved it. Julia walked away from the house, and her hand kept going back towards the dining room. The energy there wasn't right. It wasn't demonic, and it wasn't an evil spirit... but...

As Julia turned on her Jeep Wrangler, she could feel the energy radiating off that piece of mirror in her pocket.

Nothing dangerous, nothing sinister, but something…
something very, very off.

Trust your gut you fool, her aunt would say. *Trust your gut.*

It was nearing dinnertime, a time where people
didn't want solicitors at their door, but Julia felt this was
necessary.

She knew she wouldn't sleep that night if she didn't
figure this out.

As she pulled up the long driveway leading to the
Featherstone estate, she wondered what these walls must
have seen, and then she opened her mind and allowed
herself to feel it. This was one old house. People had died in
it. Not a sinister house… no poltergeists or vicious spirits
wandering around… Nothing malicious. But a place this
old had a vibration to it that she could feel.

Its history seemingly unfolded the closer she got to
it.

Two ghosts, in life a woman looking for a hair clip
before she had fallen down a flight of stairs and cracked her
neck, forever searching for the ruby hair clip. A child died
during birth. Many old men and women passed peacefully
in their beds, their spirits departed from the place
peacefully. A maid had trapped herself in the freezer
cabinet in the early 1900s and froze to death, her ghost
trapped there. A dog had been caught in the boiler room. A
man accidentally…

But nothing evil. Just the normal vibrations of things that one assumes happens in old homes. It's not just brick, stone, wood, or steel. You give these homes your life and your energy, and in the walls they are held. Julia had been places where the energies the walls held were almost impossible to stand between. Evil and malice had forced upon itself in such ways… the things that could form from this energy.

Shudder.

Julia shook herself off as she pulled the trash bag out of the seat next to her and made her way to the front steps of the house. Two giant doors with iron knockers stood before her. The old woman hadn't bothered to put in bells.

No one made houses like this anymore, fine stone mansions with a roof that was finished in a gilded fashion she had seen in a history book from the 1900s. It was as if they missed the gilded era completely and just used their money to buy big and not concentrate on the details.

The knock on the door vibrated throughout the entire house, an echo that circled about. It took a few moments, a few moments more, and Julia was about to knock again, but she felt it.

The door opened, and an old woman with white hair and gray and sagging skin on a sagging face with ancient eyes looked her up and down.

"May I help you?"

Julia pulled Mr. Chuckles from the bag, his head crushed and the rest of him burnt.

"My God!" the old woman exclaimed grabbing the doll. "Did that little boy do this to him? This was a childhood toy of mine. I loved BoJangles. His porcelain head has been smashed in. Why would they do such a thing?"

The old woman's arthritis ridden fingers reached for the string, but it had been torn off. Hurt was in her face, nostalgia coming back to her.

"I knew I should never have had that sale." The old woman shook her head, and from the stairs slowly crept down a young boy who was dressed handsomely in a little bowtie and suspenders. He looked incredibly sad, and he didn't seem phased to see the doll. "I didn't need the money, I just wanted to put a fund away for little Thomas. No one appreciates things like the owner does. The same goes for the living. Two of my children died before me in a terrible car accident leaving behind Thomas. I take care of him as if he was my own and raise him right. But... they were my children who died. Not yours. Not anyone else's. When your dog dies, people will say they are sorry. People will hug you, and they will say they understand. They don't. Someone lost only truly matters to those who have owned and lived with them, grown with them, given them your heart and parts of your life. Others don't show the same care, for they don't have the same care. They pretend with casseroles and flowers. They try to get what you are going through, but they never truly feel the hurt. They won't feel the hurt until it happens to them. My little Thomas almost got hit by a minivan on the day of the estate sale. That woman who desecrated my doll saved him, but even if she hadn't, she wouldn't have felt my pain, my loss, my suffering. She would have went on with her life, and her kids, and her job. I'd be left here with the pain. A pain only I can understand. We are selfish by nature. We only care about what is ours. Empathy is a joke of a word. They must have seen this doll as... wait... who are you?"

The old woman was nearing a hundred, and Julia understood sometimes that they go on tangents.

"I actually own a cat," Julia smiled pleasantly, but the old woman just eyed her up and down. She was also dressed in a fine gown, an old gown, but she had taken care of it. Jewels were on her neck and around her wrist. "If you don't mind, may I ask you a couple of questions?"

"I have a dinner party coming in an hour, but the maids have everything handled." The old woman shot Thomas a look as to go upstairs, but Julia quickly intervened.

"He can join us." Julia put her hand on the woman's shoulder, on her bare skin. "Please just a moment of your time."

"You are warm," the old woman gave Julia a once over, "beautiful and young. What are you twenty?"

"Yes. You have a good eye. My name is Julia Baker."

"I'm Marguerite Featherstone, and this is my grandson Thomas. You have thirty minutes before you officially become a dinner guest at this year's Reader's Digest convention. So... not to bore yourself to death, let's get this over with."

Back at the Allen residence, everything was seemingly back to normal. At such a young age, Billy couldn't comprehend anything that had just happened, almost as if his little mind blacked it out, though he did still have a slight look of fear on his face.

Wasn't a book for guiding kids through that? Patricia thought. *But my husband will distract him with video games and hugs. The best way for a child to move on from a rough spurt is through love.*

Patricia kissed Christopher on the head before leaving to pick up groceries.

"Clean that mirror up before I get back. We'll toss it on the street." She then whispered into her husband's ear, for he was playing video games with Billy, and Crystal was on the floor in the foyer aimlessly hitting Barbie and Ken together not focused on anything. "Then get that Ken doll out of her hands and dispose... no, burn it. We can go to an actual toy store with them tomorrow and get them toys that haven't been possessed."

"You ever see Chucky?" Christopher joked, and Patricia sighed and kissed him again as she grabbed her keys to head to the grocery store. Christopher yelled after her as he took a swing of his beer, "He came from a toy store! How about a Furby!?"

In the dining room, the pieces of the mirror began to shake just slightly but enough for a musical sound to vibrate throughout the house. It was a subtle sound, a sound that one who wasn't focused on something could hear. Crystal heard it in the foyer, got up, and slowly walked the yards or so through the rooms and into the dining room.

The mirror was smashed, and not a single piece of it remained in the enclosing. But under the enclosing was the same shining silver that surrounded the mirror. In the middle was a tiny mark. One would pass over it as a symbol that it was real silver; however, it was an ancient mark. An expert would know it wasn't a marking of real silver, but also wouldn't know what it was.

A voodoo practitioner would know what it was.

It was a twisted symbol used in crafts but mostly ancient voodoo.

The darkest of magic.

"That doll?" Marguerite was still annoyed at its treatment. "It was never anything but fun for me. Though it's an old, old play toy. It doesn't talk like it once did. Back in my day, these toys were colorful and new. Over the years, yes, they turn into things from horror films. But… I didn't think that nice woman would let her children treat it like this."

Julia sat for a moment. She felt bad giving the Allens a bad reputation, but trying to explain this would be… tricky.

"It certainly doesn't." Julia leaned in, "You know the Allen family… er… the family who bought the doll thought it was cursed. Had me perform an exorcism on it. They thought it was possessed. It moved around the house, and during the exorcism, it actually wrapped its hands around the little boy's neck."

"You did this? An exorcism? What are you, some sort of psychic? But, cursed?!" Marguerite waved a hand at the doll. They were in a grand living room with all old but expensive furniture and fixtures. A real fireplace crackled in the corner with iron gates in front of it. Assuming a maid would come soon to add more wood, one appeared and did. Julia was confused. "That doll gave me nothing but joy. It was that damn American Girl looking doll that was cursed. Billy was seen constantly talking to it in his room, demanding food for it, and even ordering me to leave him alone. Since she's been gone, we haven't had any trouble."

"It wasn't the doll," Thomas mumbled under his breath. "I keep telling you that Grandma."

"Well, you certainly lost your marbles when I put it out for the estate sale, and then when that little girl took it away, it was like you were losing your… a best friend."

Marguerite almost said his parents, but she caught herself, for there wasn't a mean bone in her body either. The boy had been through enough pain. Julia could sense it rising off of him. He had lost something that day. But, what?

"You did!" the boy yelled. "You gave her away!"

He got up and with tears in his eyes - mature tears, tears of someone who had lost a love - he ran up the stairs, all three flights of them, banging his feet on each step. It was the same way Billy talked in the dining room.

The mirror.

"I don't get it."

"Marguerite," Julia suddenly felt the piece of mirror in her pocket heat up. "Did you give away a mirror on that day?"

"Yes, one of my most valuable possessions. After Billy's parent's died, he moved into the room where the mirror was. A gorgeous piece of family heirloom, I found it in the attic some fifty years ago. Had it cleaned properly and hung it up in the guest room that Thomas now inhabits."

"How long have... how old is it?"

"My family originates from the boat that came before the Mayflower dear." Marguerite was obviously joking. But Julia's questions were being answered quicker than anticipated. "That mirror could be hundreds of years old for all I know. Could date back to when my family had estates in old Greece. Oh my... my guests will be arriving soon and..."

"Yes." Julia needed to get back to the Allen house immediately. It was a thirty minute drive, but she would speed. Damn, she wouldn't speed. There were cops on the road; she felt it. "Thank you so much for your time, Mrs. Featherstone. Hope you have a grand party."

Marguerite Featherstone had a great party, and her grandson cried over his loss in his bedroom the entire time. Staring at the wall where the mirror hung. Crying like a man who had just lost his wife.

Get something sharp
Get something to bleed
Open your skin
Drop it onto me
Get something sharp
Get something to bleed
Open your skin
Drop it onto me

Three year old Crystal found a pair of new scissors and had them in her hands and was standing over the mirror. Her tiny face stared into the silver and the symbol at the middle of it. She was transfixed on it. It glowed and pulsated as a heart would. Slow beats, slow rhythms. The voice in her head, singing sweet songs, musical rules to follow.

Got something sharp
Got something to bleed
Open your skin
Drop it onto me
Got something sharp
Got something to bleed
Open your skin
Drop it onto me

Crystal's eyes were glossed over. A three year old, a little girl who hadn't even begun to live yet, dressed in the cutest dress her mother had bought her a few weeks ago, a dress she thought her daughter would look great in for Thanksgiving dinner. Crystal instead insisted on wearing it around. Crystal loved dresses, and she loved to spin in them with her Barbies and dance around the house. Every morning Patricia would do her hair, and they would giggle together. Patricia would pretend to put makeup on her face as Crystal idolized how her mother made her face up.

Got something sharp
Got something to bleed
Open your skin
Drop it onto me
Got something sharp
Got something to bleed
Open your skin
Drop it onto me

Crystal tilted her head slightly, took the scissors and raised them directly in front of her. Both her hands were gripping the handle tight, the pointed end facing her small body. In the other room, Billy yelled as his dad beat him in Mario Kart - Christopher had mastered the game some time ago. He'd let his son win for a while, but then he'd pick Peach and own him on every level. Gotta teach them how life is both fair and unfair.

Got something sharp
Got something to bleed
Open your skin
Drop it onto me
Got something sharp
Got something to bleed
Open your skin
Drop it onto me

Crystal raised the scissors slowly, the flicker of sharpness reflecting off the chandelier in the dining room. Billy yelled at his dad and said he demanded no more games, and he was hungry. Christopher told him one more because he had to let the kid win the final race. He picked Bowser, and Billy picked Toad and then Rainbow Road. His dad let out a hefty sigh as no one likes Rainbow Road.

Crystal went to bring the scissors down into her chest.

STOP.

A drop.

Prick your finger.

A drop in the center.

Prick your finger.

STOP.

Only a drop.

Crystal pricked her finger and a single drop of blood fell from her hand onto the mirror. The video game was so loud in the 'man cave' they couldn't hear the orgasmic sound the mirror made, the releasing of sexual tension so intense it outdid any porn you could ever imagine. Crystal's eyes returned to normal, and she stumbled back into the corner to watch as the mirror began to shoot light directly toward the ceiling.

Gold seemingly began to pour out of the center of the mirror, gold mixed with sparkles with brilliant colors that were exquisite as if the richest of diamonds were pouring out of the mirror in a flooding form.

They all began to swirl together.

The colors, the brilliance, the diamonds, the gold.

A figure began to form out of it in the center of the mirror from the symbol in the center.

A small flash of light.

Crystal smiled brighter than she had ever smiled before. As far as she was concerned, a Disney Princess was in front of her.

The goddess looking woman was stretching her arms high and yawning as if she had been asleep for the longest time. Her skin glowed and sparkled, and her body was covered in a shawl of diamonds that seemingly bounced in air. Her hair was gold and strung up upon itself in a Greek fashion with diamonds and gold gems along it. Her face young… and must we repeat, beautiful.

The minute she stepped out of the mirror, all the glitter dropped from her, all the sparkle and glow, all the goddess like aspects.

"Curses," she said. "I'm sorry for this. Time to refresh myself.."

The beautiful creature closed her eyes. Breathing in heavily, Crystal was scared for a second but nothing was happening to her. She saw in the corner that the plants were dying, and she could smell food going rotten in the kitchen. Lawns and bushes died, flowers wilted, and trees that had stood for hundreds of years were desecrated. Bugs dropped by the millions as their life force was sucked out of them.

"My name is Cassiopeia." The beautiful creature smiled at Crystal. The glow had returned to her softer than when she first came out of the mirror. She looked around at the place, studying everything with her golden diamond eyes. "I am not in Greece anymore, am I? Time to learn. Time to grow. Time to shine. Time to glow."

"You…" Crystal was wide eyed, "you are beautiful."

"I know." Cassiopeia's facial expression didn't change as she looked around. "I know."

As outside lights came quickly swirling on - she looked terrified - she swirled her hands about each other, spinning and evaporating in a splash and sparkle of gold. A slight orgasmic sound followed her as she vanished, a release.

Crystal sat there with her mouth open. She had sat in front of princess and fairy movies, but she had just met, as far as she was concerned, the queen of all the fairies. She would never forget this... ever. Not now in 1997, and not later... when she would encounter Cassiopeia again.

The lights were from Patricia's car returning home from the store.

At the same time, though, Julia Baker's jeep came speeding to a stop. She ran up the stairs and began banging on the door. Her heart pounding her chest, sweat breaking at her brow, she had tied her red hair back and had driven at such a speed, as to not get pulled over, but she was so worried for...

"Hello." Crystal smiled, a pair of scissors in her hands, a small blood spot on one of her fingers. "The fairy princess is gone."

Julia stepped into the house and surveyed it faster than she had ever surveyed a house before. The boys were in another match of Mario Kart, and the house was in one piece. She turned to the dining room, across from which Patricia stepped out and startled said, "Julia, did you forget something?"

"It was the mirror." Julia walked into the dining room and pointed down at the mirror. "It was the mirror that made the doll come to life. It was the mirror both Billy and Thomas were talking to. I walked by it, and I saw myself more beautiful than I ever had before."

Patricia wasn't looking at her like she was crazy, which was a good sign,

"I walked by it too… on my way to work this morning… and thought I had never looked so good either." Patricia noticed her daughter holding the sharp scissors. "Crystal! What are you doing? Why are you playing with those? What happened to her finger? Did you see?"

"I just got here."

"It was a fairy princess Mommy." Crystal pointed over to where the mirror was laying on the floor. Both Patricia and Julia noticed that all the broken pieces were gone. All that was left was a silver oval, but it seemed tarnished now, next week's junk. "A drop of my blood. She rose out of waves of sparkles. She glowed Mommy, she glowed. Can I meet Santa Clause next?"

Julia could also smell rotting food. She went to the window and noticed as far as she could see all the plants were dead. All the lawns were rotted. All the trees had died. No… this wasn't a demon. Her aunt had once told her a story of a woman who possessed so much beauty she was praised wherever she want, and got whatever she want. Her aunt had said it was her power. Underneath it all she was a witch, a special one. Though she shimmered in diamonds in Greece, claiming sacrifices and accepting offerings that had brought her to her most powerful state, claiming to be a goddess, a blood trail had followed her, as it had once before… her name had been… had been…

"Crystal, dear," Julia couldn't hide the worry on her face, "do you remember her name"

For, not all monsters were ugly.

"Cassi… Cassia… Cassieee…"

"Cassopeia." Julia looked outside at all the dead that was around, "You and your family are fine Patricia. The mirror was holding something. Get rid of everything you got at that yard sale, and never go to one again. Stick to the park longer next time. I'm sorry, but I need to go."

Julia was lost in thought as she aimlessly made her way to her car. Starting it up, she recalled how her aunt had told her much more about this creature. A sorceresses more than a witch, quite like her aunt. But she needed to know more.

Go home, her gut told her. *Go to your Aunt Gwen.*

Monster

Winter, 2015

Rich was at a bar with his cousin and brother.

An old dive just down the street from where they worked, a central location for the business locale to go for happy hour, and then at a certain time, the chairs were cleared and a dance floor appeared turning the place into a night club. The lights would go red, and the entire ambiance would change. A drink cost fifteen bucks, but it was worth it for the bar was convenient and local.

Every time the door opened, a light gust of wind and snow came in with it. It had been a struggle of a day at the office, which was expected when you work with your immediate family; each day was eggshells and lies. The stress of it all was getting to him, and trying to make enough money to pay all the bills, the mortgage, and car payments was causing him to actually work, and not vanish at lunch hours or skip days all together.

Rich liked to do what he wanted when he wanted. The selfish mind of a child one would say, but the true dream goal of others. However, no one can actually live life that way.

"Yup. That's enough beers. It's time to get home," his brother said. "New born and a three year old, she'll kill me if I start smelling like liquor and a bar. I better not brush up against any women on my way out. Ha. If I ever cheated on her, she'd smell the perfume from the woman a mile away. She'd be waiting at the door with an axe. But, that's why you get married, so things like that don't happen. Right?"

"Right," his cousin said, who was just tired from the amount of pain pills he had taken that day. It was an addiction, but it didn't affect his work and was for some reason a topic the family didn't need to bring up. "Rich, did you want..."

"Seriously?" Rich raised his eyebrow as it was rare his cousin actually offered to share his pain killers, "Yah I'll take one."

"I hate how you two exchange drugs like candy," his brother said while wrapping his scarf around his neck and pulling his ski hat over his hair. "Rich you could get addicted to those things. You already miss enough work. Do you really need to add a pill addiction to your list?"

"And I'm not?" their cousin said, with a growl in his voice, as he passed along the pill to Rich. "Send me to rehab, or just drop the topic. I don't bother you about your life things."

Their brother pushed his drink away.

"Because my life is in order. Mixing the two substances doesn't make you pleasant to be around either. I don't know why we do these happy-hours because they are never happy or fun with either of you." He looked at Rich. "Are you coming? The roads are just going to get worse as this storm continues, and you don't want to get stuck in the city or the inevitable minivan that'll cause an accident near the bridge. Dad's getting annoyed at you charging random hotel rooms on the company card."

"Just go. I just want one more drink." Rich, sliding the pill in his jacket pocket, let off his smile, which closed so many deals. But his brother saw right through and shook his head. "I'll save that for a rainy day."

"See you tomorrow then," his cousin said awkwardly patting him on the back before putting his own heavy coat on. "Half day Friday?"

"That's a joke," his brother said. "Dad never gives us half anything. See yah tomorrow Rich. Don't drink too much. I know today was rough, but you are the one who keeps saying he's going to write a resume up and find another job. You are starting to sound like a record on repeat, so either shit or get off the pot. No one is forcing you to work for the group."

"I know. I know." Rich swung back the vodka soda. "Goodnight guys. Text me in the morning if you want coffee or breakfast. I'll pick it up on the way to work. Have good nights."

They left. Rich looked at his phone and hadn't received any texts, messages, or even work related emails. He didn't have many friends, and if his cousin and brother wouldn't go out drinking with him, he would probably be out drinking by himself. But tonight, he didn't feel like leaving the bar alone. He looked at his phone again forgetting he meant to look at the time in the first place. It was close to ten, meaning...

The lights began to lower, and the red uplighting from behind the couches and along the ceiling came on. The owner of this place must have gotten to know his customers and know the type of area he was in. Catch the business newbies with the money during happy hour, and catch the girls getting free drinks from the single men after the lights went low.

Rich took the painkiller out of his pocket, popped it in his mouth, and ordered a tequila shot. He was out of his comfort zone and didn't do well without some sort of substance in him. He probably smoked way too much weed, and anytime his cousin offered him a pill he'd snatch one up. Each day he would try and sneak one or two out of his bottle.

Being shy and awkward was his norm and not exactly what women wanted from a man in a bar. He just didn't feel like leaving alone tonight.

Liquid and RX courage.

The bartenders had switched. The one during the daytime was your typical 'come complain to me about work' fifty something year old man with a beard and a sincere expression for all your problems. The one at night was a buff, over six feet tall hunk with devilish eyes and a shirt that his muscles had issues not ripping the seams from. Rich looked him over. God was he attractive. But Rich didn't have it in him to even talk to him let alone let the hunk know he was also into men.

He had been working under his father for years and made all his money through that. He talked timelessly about writing up a resume and finding a new job. Make his own money and not just take it from his family, which was almost like an allowance when it really came down to it. But daddy's money kept on flowing, and Rich in no way was stuck. He was just comfortable… As his brother said, 'comfortable complaining.'

Rich didn't have it in him to go to a gay bar. He had experimented with his cousin when he was younger, something that had went on for a few years. He lost his virginity to him, and it had been his first real sexual experience. His cousin claimed it was kids being kids, but Rich knew he had to have enjoyed it. Though now, his cousin popped pills like candy and had issues meeting Rich in the eye.

He loved it, Rich thought about a night they had spent together at fifteen, *just as much as I did.*

Though he didn't have it in him to bring it up again, for fear of him confirming his fears. It was just kids being kids.

Rich didn't have it in him to do a lot of things.

However, Rich had it in him to take a pill, take a shot of liquor, and attempt to pick up a girl tonight. He would have never been able to do it sober; he just didn't have that high of self-esteem. His hair was thinning on the top of his head, he hadn't hit the gym in a while, and forgetting his contacts was a norm these day. He always felt like a nerd in his glasses. He also hadn't shaven properly in a while. All those little details that if tended to would spawn more of an attractive person.

A couple of college girls had taken the stools next to him. Rich, himself, was going to hit thirty this year, and they were obviously a bunch of typical first or second year sorority chicks, but sometimes…

"Hey man," Rich called to the bartender and slipped a hundred dollar bill on the table, "whatever these lovely ladies want get it for them."

"Sure." The bartender raised an eyebrow, and Rich saw just how green his eyes were and was wondering what he looked like without his shirt on. "Ladies this gentleman…"

"Oh my God, Chelsea," the first attractive collegial student said to the other as she turned towards Rich. Even though it was thirty degrees out, she was in a skirt and loose blouse, "That was easier than I thought it would be. Hi, I'm Kelsey."

Easier than I thought as well, flew through Rich's mind. *Maybe tonight is my lucky night.*

"I'm Rich. Well I'm not rich, but my name is Rich." The pill hadn't kicked in, and he was stammering over his words already, "Whatever you ladies want is on me."

"How sweet of you," Kelsey placed a hand on his shoulder, and tingles rushed through his body. Human contact was a necessity for him at points. He felt human contact was a necessity for all. "Well, Chelsea write it down. Within five minutes we got a stranger to put down a hundred bucks and told us to order whatever we want."

"Got it! No way the other team can beat that." Chelsea began typing on her iPhone and looked at the other two girls they were with, "At this rate we will win in no time."

"I think we have time to spend this hundred though," their friend the farthest down at the bar called to the bartender. "Your most expensive shots! Let's do this quick! Seriously, be creative and make us something that glows or tastes like chocolate cake."

The hunky bartender smiled and winked at the girls as if he knew exactly what they wanted. Did he know exactly what they wanted? Was he one of those guys who could pick up any girl and know exactly what would make them smile, blush, or giggle? He probably was.

"Quick? Team?" Rich was confused. The bartender used the entire hundred Rich had put down and poured out three shots for each of the four girls, and they shimmered. What was it? Liquid gold? "Don't I get a…?"

But before he could even get the words out, the girls did one shot after the other until they were gone. They began to put their North Face coats back on and scarves around their neck. Kelsey kissed Rich on the cheek, and he took this as an invitation to join them.

"Where we heading off to?"

The girls all looked at each other and laughed, and Chelsea looked at Rich with the most pitiful look he had received that night. A dog at the pound who was being sent to its slaughter. Kelsey smiled that smile Rich had seen when a client liked you but didn't want to close the deal with you,

"Oh baby," Kelsey's hand was on Rich's chest, "we didn't come out to meet people. Our sorority is on a scavenger hunt. One of the things on the list was to get a guy to buy you a drink at a bar. What were the specifics, Chelsea?"

"How long we were at the bar. How much he spent on the drinks. How old he was."

"That's right. We were here for two minutes, one hundred dollars…" Kelsey turned back to Rich with her hand still on his chest, which she wasn't even feeling. The only part of his body that really still had some muscle to it. "How old are you?"

"I am 29."

Kelsey's eyes went up and down him as her hand fell from his chest.

"You are only 29? I would've guessed…" But she giggled from the three shots she just took down, "Gosh what stress must do to a person. I'll keep that in mind. Are you a smoker?"

"Yes." Rich quickly reached into his jacket pocket for a cigarette. "Want to have one with me before you ladies leave?"

They all giggled at once together, and Rich felt that void in him. There were only so many times an ego could be bruised.

"Note to all," Chelsea said from behind Kelsey, "heavy drinking and smoking leads to looking like you are almost forty at thirty."

"Chelsea."

"Oh, come on Kelsey. We'll never see him again." Kelsey took Chelsea's hand and smiled half politely at Rich. But in her eyes was the *its time to go* look. "Thanks for helping us with our scavenger hunt. You probably are the reason we'll win this year, but that's all you are getting from us tonight."

"I'm sorry," Kelsey said to Rich, and in her eyes she meant it. But in her eyes were pity. Pity for a man who didn't look his age sitting at a bar alone spending a hundred bucks on a bunch of girls who literally needed to check something off a list. "She's a little harsh after a couple drinks. But, seriously, thank you. I hope you find... whatever it is you are looking for."

In a twirl of sweet perfume and luscious hair, the girls were gone and out of the bar before Rich could even say goodbye. The bartender looked at him with a smirk as he sat back against the bar, and Rich's eye fell to his groin, which the bartender caught, humorously. Even if the hunk was gay, they were in two very different leagues.

"Another tequila shot," Rich said trying to avoid the natural bulge of the bartender's jeans. He put another hundred on the table. "Now. Please. Just keep them coming."

"Whatever it is you are looking for, eh? You sure you are in the right bar, sir?"

Sir.

"Just drinks." He wanted to add the word asshole, but he didn't have that in him either. He wasn't one for confrontation. He didn't like to argue or fight, and he definitely needed substances in him to even speak back to someone. He'd rather lie than have a tough conversation with someone. He'd rather smile and say everything was ok.

His brain spun. The pill was settling in and so were the tequila shots, but when you are not in the right frame of mind mentally, that's not always a good thing. He had started with beer, had some mixed drinks, and now tequila shots. *Beer before liquor, never sicker, rang in his head, but had they fractioned painkillers into that mix?*

At most, he thought, he'd find a girl, buy her a drink, and spend a night flirting, which could potentially lead to sex. Yes, sex. Meaningless sex. Just some human interaction and a one-on-one connection even if it wasn't going to be a repeated act. Even if he never saw her again. A one-night stand would be nice.

He wasn't exactly off to a good start.

The first girl he met tonight used him. Rich didn't care how her or her friends phrased it. He just got used by a bunch of sorority girls; he was a check on a list on a scavenger hunt. Next the bartender caught him checking him out, and he obviously wasn't into it. Why would he be? He was over six feet tall and could have played Superman. Last week Rich had to go up a pants size, and his dress shirts weren't hiding his beer gut, especially when he was sitting down.

He felt his phone vibrate in his pocket, looked at his iWatch, and hit ignore. He raised his hand, and the bartender actually sent the bus boy down to serve him his next drink. Great, the bartender was genuinely creeped out by him.

10pm turned into 11pm, which turned close to midnight. All around him were people laughing and telling jokes, stories of their days, making fun of their bosses, discussing the circus that this upcoming election was. He had turned his phone off to make it stop vibrating and kept taking shot after shot. He was definitely high and could have used another pill, but he felt somewhat good.

He just wished…

One of these groups were his. One of these groupings of friends talking and laughing and joking wanted to have him involved. The only words spoken to him between when those sorority girls left and the bartender caught him staring at his junk was when some guy asked him to move over so he and his friends could sit. Rich obliged. Though he wanted to say no, he couldn't because he just didn't have it in him.

It didn't even need to be a big group. Just a couple of people who weren't his family members who would come out and have a few drinks with him. Maybe a girl who flirted with him and they fooled around occasionally. Or a boy who would brush his leg in private and…

"Hey man." A handsome guy was next to him. A blonde hair, flashy eyed stud, who obviously was in the gym daily and was dressed so nice. That wasn't all; he could feel it. He felt the gay vibe off of him. "How's it going tonight? Having fun?"

"Great!" Rich let out a smile that he had learned over the years. That salesman smile no one said no to, and at one point during college had let him in many a girl's pants. "I'm Rich. My name is Rich. I'm not actually rich. If you don't mind me saying… wait… let me start again. Can I buy you a drink?"

"Me?" The guy laughed, and behind him a group of friends were there. "No. I'm good. But do you mind if we take your stool? The rest of my friends are at the bar, and you are kind of in the middle of it all."

He was right. He was in the middle between one big group of friends. All well-dressed attractive male and females drinking and laughing and catching up. He was literally the loner and was blocking the stool from this attractive guy who was obviously gay.

Rich leaned a little closer, the pills and liquor combining,

"Maybe you want to go to the bathroom with me? Or out to my car for a little bit?"

The guy's eyebrows raised.

"I have a boyfriend, man." He looked Rich over. The thinning hair, the gut, the badly taken care of beard and the pale skin with the druggie eyes. "Plus. Learn to play in your league. I'm sure you'll find someone who is on your par. Maybe hit the gym a little bit. Or try Club-Z, a gay bar down…"

Rich just got up and raised a hand.

"Stop. Please, I get it."

He grabbed his coat, took his last shot of tequila, and went back to where the red couches were. It was a completely empty part of the bar at this point. It was not the point of the night where people needed to sit down because they were so drunk. Couples weren't breaking off to make out yet, and people weren't making drunken best friends. Plus, they didn't do bottle service on the weekdays. On the weekends, you had to rent these couches, and a group of friends could drink and hang out all night long.

Rich couldn't even do that if he wanted to. He didn't have the friends to fill a couple bar stools, let alone get bottle service. Sigh.

He slumped down into a couch and looked back over at the bar. The gay guy had whispered into all his friends' ears, and they were all looking back at Rich with pity and amusement. Who asks a random guy to go into the bathroom with him? To go out to the car with him? The next thing Rich saw was an attractive blonde telling the bartender what happened, and the bartender pointed at his junk. Rich knew he was telling him that he was staring at it after trying to pick up girls.

Pity. Pitiful. Pathetic. Positively painful.

It normally doesn't go like this, right? People normally will respond with some humanity. You can normally find someone to converse with.

"For so much positive energy in this place, why do you look so sad?" the vixenish female voice asked. Rich hadn't noticed anyone sitting back there when he moved. But he had been so embarrassed by the previous encounters of the night that he was all up in his mind and hadn't noticed.

Her.

Eyes were dark but glistened and a light aqua dust of shine was spread across her lids, and her long lashes fluttered every time she blinked. Onyx hair wrapped up stylishly, pale skin almost like the snow, blue luscious lips, and high cheek bones. Her body could have been featured in a Victoria Secret's ad. She was poised against the red leather couch like she was on a photo shoot, a tight black sheer dress with blue highlights covered her body to knees, where long legs in fishnets ended in dark blue high heel stilettos with long thin points at the end of them. A metal necklace that didn't match her outfit - chain links - wrapped her neck and fell into her perfect bosoms where enough cleavage showed to make Rich's pants instantly tighten.

She held up a hand, and Rich instantly took it. It was cold. She must have just come in.

"Rich," he stammered. "I'm not rich that's just my name."

"Mia." Her laugh was light and warming, like the smile that spread across her face. "That was clever. It's always attractive when a man can be clever. Wit and charm normally go hand in hand."

"Can I get you a drink?" Rich was trying to take in everything he was seeing, but it was impossible. Maybe the pill he had taken was in full effect, and maybe he was so drunk that this woman wasn't as attractive as she seemed. But this was reality. He didn't need to pinch himself or wake up. "What do you drink?"

"Surprise me," Mia smiled. "Surprises are always so much fun. What's the fun in knowing everything that's going to happen?"

Rich stumbled back to the bar and was face to face with the huge hunky bartender whose bulge had been violated by Rich's eyes not moments ago.

"Two long island iced teas please." Rich tossed a couple twenties down on the counter. He wanted to get back to the couches before Mia was noticed by anyone else. "Quick."

The bartender slowly looked over to where he had come from and raised an eyebrow. He was obviously impressed at what he was seeing. How could he not be? This was a true spitfire.

"Looks like your luck turned around, sir." The bartender turned to make the drinks. Sir… they had to be the same age or around that. Yet, Rich had gotten a sir. But, Mia had chosen him, had chosen to talk to him, out of everyone in this bar, including the bartender. There she sat waiting for her drink. Maybe Rich was too hard on his appearance. They always say you can never truly see yourself. "Here you go, sir."

As he passed by the blonde gay guy and his gaggle of friends, they all giggled as they had obviously been making fun of him for trying to get their friend into the bathroom. But right now Rich didn't care. Right now his focus was on Mia.

"LIT," Rich put the drink down on the small glass table in front of them, "a little bit of everything."

"A LIT." Mia took a sip of the drink through the straw, "Interesting name for a drink, don't you think? A Long Island Iced Tea. Ever wonder if the people on Long Island came up with it, or because of how crazy those areas can be they named the strongest drink possible after it? I wonder if the people on Long Island call it something different or if they revel in the fact that a blackout drink was named after their tiny island."

"I'm not trying to get you drunk," Rich quickly stammered. He was - he hoped she didn't think he was, though.

"Oh." Mia laughed and took another sip, "It takes more than one drink to affect me like that. Relax into this atmosphere. We are at a place where people go to laugh and enjoy themselves. You seem so tense."

Mia brought a soft hand across Rich's hand, smiled at him, and met his eyes.

"So for besides being Rich who isn't rich, tell me about yourself."

Her hand didn't move from his.

"I… own my company actually. Single. Live outside the city in New Jersey. Have a golden retriever. Also have a flat here in the city for nights like this. Love to hike and go on adventures, camp with my friends. I spend a lot of time with my friends when I'm not at work. We go out to places like this all the time and go on vacations together. Actually just gave an employee a big promotion, which is why I came out celebrating tonight. They all actually just left when I came and sat by you. I was about to call one of my friends to join me, but you are plenty of company. I'll call… Joe on another night."

Rich was used to convincing people in his job to give them their money, so he was used to twisting the truth a little bit. Own his own company, right. Even if his father retired, he'd hand everything to his brother who didn't have drug and drinking issues and who didn't show up and leave work every day early. Also, he had no friends as people just didn't seem to enjoy his company after a while. But, '*I work for my father at the bottom of the employee chain, have no friends, and don't take work seriously*' isn't how you impress anyone… let alone a woman like Mia.

"What a life you have, Rich." Mia kept her smile and batted her eyelashes, "What a fulfilling and happy life. One of the lucky ones, as they would say, someone who doesn't have to worry about tomorrow because they have everything today."

He pulled his hand away from hers and brought it to his drink.

"Tell me a little about you, Mia. Where are you from? Do I detect an accent?"

"You do." Mia unfolded her long legs and recrossed them so one of her legs was now up against Rich's leg. "I am my own boss, and I have been for what feels like forever. I travel a lot for work. I've been to New York City more times than I can count as well as other cities around this world. I am also single. Traveling so much makes it very hard to keep a solid connection in one place. Though it seems in each city I find a man who wants more, but you can only give so much when you are constantly moving around. I'm sure you understand?"

Rich couldn't believe what he was hearing as she brought her leg up and down his. It was in slow motions, and she was brushing against him. Sexually. He couldn't stand right now because through his slacks another small embarrassment would probably be popping up...

"No husband, anywhere?"

"On another planet perhaps." Mia let out a laugh that had a slight cackle to it. "What is the point of getting married if you aren't going to be around? What is the point of telling someone 'always and forever' if 'always and forever' means probably never? The cruelest thing one can do is play with another's heart. I don't believe in cruelty. Do you?"

"No," Rich said too quickly. "I don't believe in cruelty."

Her hand was back on his shoulder, and it crept to his neck, just enough so her nails could rub against the back of his head.

"You didn't come here tonight to leave alone, did you?"

"No."

"Close out your tab." Mia ran her nails back away from Rich's neck, and he yearned to be touched by her again. "Let's go elsewhere. I'm sure you've found what you've been looking for here."

"I..." Rich knew he was drunk and high, and when this happened, he couldn't always perform. Viagra would come in handy right about now. He was so nervous and so drunk and so high. This could turn into another embarrassment, and he wasn't sure he could handle not being able to satisfy this beautiful woman, this Mia. "Are you sure?"

"Close out your tab, and meet me outside." Mia let out that smile again, and Rich bounced off the couch. The bar was now completely crowded, and he had to push through people to get to the hunk of a man who was bartending. He made sure it was him he finished the night off with. He wanted him to see his trophy he was bringing out.

"Close out my tab."

"You've been paying in cash, sir." The bartender

watched, and so did all the men as Mia moved through the crowd, which parted as she made her way towards the front door. Rich turned towards the bartender, and it was the liquor and drugs, but gave him a smug smile.

"Guess I've been in the right place all along."

"Tell yourself whatever you want, sir. I've worked with people long enough to know what I see and what I know. A woman like that could have anyone she wanted. She picked you. You who tried to get a random gay guy into the bathroom with you and have been raping me with your eyes all night. You who turned your phone off hours ago and have been drinking alone."

Rich just stared at him, and his eyes did run along his pants one more time.

"My point exactly, so go. Have fun with one of the finest women of the night. I'll make a bet she's a prostitute, and you are going to wind up paying in one form or another tonight. We all get what we deserve. So go. Go along. Get what you deserve."

"You aren't getting a tip," was the cleverest thing Rich could think of. "I'll give this place a terrible review on Yelp."

"You aren't getting my tip either." The bartender laughed, and so did everyone who heard that. Rich turned bright red and went towards the door. Putting his jacket on upside down causing half the bar to laugh at him, he finally figured it out - how to put a jacket on properly - and wrapped his scarf around his neck and put his gloves on.

Stay calm. Just. Stay calm.

Mia waited outside, letting the snow and cold air flow over her, as it was way too warm in that bar. She heard someone spit behind her. It didn't make her jump because Mia didn't scare easily. Turning on her heels was a woman neither young nor old, with hair in dreads filled with gems and stones of various strings of colors. A tanned face with sparkling eyes, covered in layers upon layers of real furs. Furs from various countries, various times, and various creatures. Stories behind each of them, Mia was sure. The energy that radiated off of her could have melted the snow. Mia immediately noticed the snow wasn't spinning about her and that she was completely dry, and the wind didn't affect her hair or clothes.

"You leave no footprints in the snow. Dressed like that anyone would be shivering, but you seem… comfortable," the woman said to Mia, running her eyes over her. "What business of yours is here?"

Mia studied the woman for a second, smelled her, and knew.

"Witch?"

"I prefer Gwen."

"Gwen?! Really? My lucky night!" Mia smiled an actual bright smile with the dark blue lips as the snow gust about her. "Gwendala, the infamous swamp witch. You are famed throughout our community. I must say, how you got that serial killer demon out of your body is a story I would love to hear. I've heard rumors but that power! Your battle with the voodoo priest, that demon child you helped give birth to. Is it true you were able to remove the demon from that child, and it lived a healthy life?! Oh if I could just taste that power!"

"I prefer Gwen. But, would you?" Gwen inquired eying Mia over. "If we were alone in a room, would it be a fight, or would it be civility?"

"Civility. I couldn't even imagine... I mean you are a superstar," Mia said with honesty. She was gazing upon a legend. "What brings you to this 'big apple?' How did you... how did you find me?"

"This is just a stopping ground. I'm heading west. But... I know the smell of one of you by this point. I know the smell of all of them by this point." Gwen's face became very stern for a moment. "You know... I could vanquish you..."

Mia did not doubt that for a second.

"That's not necessary, just wait," Mia said. "Give him time to come out."

"After he comes out? Then what? No mortal can hurt me. If you know who I am you know what I am capable of."

"Just wait a moment Gwen." Mia put a hand on the witch's face. "We aren't all monsters."

Gwen looked Mia up and down, allowing her energy to run through her, judging her, and nodded with a hmph.

"Fine, whatever."

Rich exited the bar and saw Mia and a woman whose age he could not detect. She was definitely a beautiful creature, but his eyes never left Mia to look her over long enough.

Rich approached the two, "A friend of yours?"

"An idol of mine actually." Mia spread her arms, "Gwen this is Rich. He was kind enough to buy me a drink at the bar tonight. Remove your glove and shake her hand, Rich. It's not polite to shake a woman's hand gloved."

Rich had never heard that before, but he wasn't about to argue with Mia. He took off his glove and shook the woman's hand. Gwen looked him up and down, breathing him in, and then a look of understanding flashed in her eyes.

Threesome, Rich thought hopefully, *cause that'd be awesome.*

"Rich," Gwen took her hand back, disgusted, "kind of you to offer my friend a drink. At a bar. How original. True kindness is rare these days. Now go get the woman a taxi! She's barely wearing anything, and you haven't even offered her your coat! Bah. Is chivalry dead? Sho! Sho!"

Rich went to the corner, and Gwen turned towards Mia.

"We all have to do what we have to in order to survive." Mia's smile was gone, but her face was still beautiful and pleasant. "I just choose…"

"…I get it." Gwen looked her over once more and took a step back. "You are an old one aren't you? You are as old as time. The younger ones are stupid and deserve to be vanquished by any witch or hunter that passes their way. But you…"

"Shall we meet again?"

"We both have long lives ahead of us," Gwen said as she put a fur hood over her head. "I'm heading West…"

"So am I." Mia raised her shoulders and smiled as if they were the oldest of friends. "You must know what's coming upon us. California is my final destination."

Gwen turned, and all of the snow around her exploded away in a throttle of energy.

"California?" Gwen was right up against Mia. "Tell me you aren't allowing them…"

"No," Mia look a step back from the witch, "I'm going to stop them."

"As am I." Gwen looked Mia over with approval. "For what you are… you have empathy."

"Some could say the same thing about you, witch."

Mia turned as Rich finally hailed a cab and was calling her over.

"Maybe let's travel to California together. We could help each other out. Plus, I'd truly love to hear the story of how you got that child killing demon out of your body. Maybe teach me a thing or two about avoiding possession…"

But when Mia turned, Gwen was gone.

In California, Mia thought, *we shall meet again. For a war that will shake the foundation of this planet.*

Mia approached Rich and the cab. She didn't have a coat on or anything and just stood there as the snow gust about her, her eyes on Rich.

"Aren't you cold?" Rich was shivering. "It has to be below thirty. Here take my jacket."

"I don't get cold," Mia smiled and motioned for him to follow her. "Must be something in my genes, but even in the coldest of winters I find myself fine. It's the heat that bothers me. Always has."

"Where yah guys going?" the cabbie asked. Meter already running, impatience in his voice, he didn't even bother to look back at them.

Mia looked over at Rich for a moment.

"Your place?" Mia asked, knowing he didn't actually have a flat in the city. "What's the address?"

"I have roommates at my flat in the city," Rich said too quickly. "Be a little awkward to explain... to well... to..."

"Then to my place." Mia gave the cab driver the address of the upper east side, near central park, where brownstones and fancy apartments were. Where the upper crust sent their children to private schools and crime was at a low.

"You live here?" Rich's eyes were spread open at the brownstone they were pulling up to. "This is... I've never... I've never been in one of these."

"Well tonight you will be." Mia looked over at Rich

who was stumbling to pull his wallet out and pay the cab driver, "I got this ride. You can get out."

"Are you sure?"

"Hush. You paid for drinks, so I'll cover the cab. Let's go dutch tonight." Mia smiled and waited for Rich to leave the car. She put her hand through the sliding non-smash glass and touched the back of the cab driver's head. "You've been paid and tipped heavily. Go home and be faithful to your wife, text your secret girlfriend right now, and break it off with her. Tell her your wife found out, and you can't live in this lie anymore because you can't. Because it's cruel to play with someone's heart."

The cab driver just sat there for a moment, his eyes closing as if he was going to fall asleep - then they burst open and...

"Thank you for the great tip, miss," the cab driver said before switching his cab off duty. He pulled out his cellphone and began to text furiously. "Thank you."

He owes me more than he knows, Mia thought, *more than he knows.*

Rich was staring at the three-floor brownstone. It was ancient, one of the first of the real wealth to be built in the city. Mia had kept it up over the years, assuring that with time and as fashions changed, so did her place. She would have preferred a corner one, but at that time she was lucky to get this one, being a woman.

"What exactly is it that you do?" Rich was slightly awestruck as Mia keyed the code in the door for it slide open. "I mean... I own my own company and only have a flat in the city and own a large house in New Jersey."

More lies.

"I've been in trades and sales," Mia stepped into the foyer of her grand brownstone, "for what feels like forever."

That was not a lie.

Mia switched on the lights, and Rich let out a sound of awe. Men were always impressed by wealth and shiny things, and Mia's brownstone was just that. A chandelier from Italy hung in the foyer, and a statue from China under a staircase twirled to a second and third floor. The stones on the floor were flown in from Italy. The entire place was fractions and pieces of different cultures, civilizations, and times all put together to create one work of art.

"So." Mia walked into the living room, furs on the floor, couches of fine material. Various sculptures and from what Rich could swear was an original Picasso on the wall. "You are single?"

"I… am," Rich smiled. "How about another drink. I'm sorry, but… how my night started and how it's ending seems to be a mind-fuck… I mean mind-tease… I mean mind…"

"I know what you mean." Mia took strides across the room to multi glass shelving that held various liquor bottles and various glasses. "Life is a funny thing isn't it? We leave work thinking we are going to have a couple of drinks with our cousin and our brother. We get made fun of by college girls, and gay guys, and the bartender… yet you wind up in the fanciest house you have ever seen with the most beautiful woman you have ever laid eyes on."

Rich's mouth fell open slightly. Hadn't he told her he was out with friends celebrating a coworker's promotion?

Nor did he mention any of the embarrassment he received from the bartender, the college girls, or his pathetic attempt at getting that cute gay guy to give him a hand job in a car. Or did he? He was pretty drunk, and it had been a few days since he had taken any drugs. Confession always come out when you are…

"Drunk. Intoxicated. Annihilated. Mentally away. At one point in time, the Greeks thought that blacking out was reaching their gods, that the more intoxicated they got, the closer they were brought and elevated towards the higher beings." Mia was seated next to him on the couch. "Rich, who is not rich, which is a pickup line that will work on no one, ever. Do you find me attractive?"

Was this a game? Was this a hidden camera reality show? Was a curtain going to fall with cameras appearing? Would he get a check for a few thousand to play along? A blind man could find a way to find Mia attractive, not just attractive but hot, steamy hot. She wasn't Disney princess beautiful; she was a pure vixen with her dark glistening eyes, almost translucent skin, and dark blue lips. The ways her eyes fluttered and lashes beat, as if to some song or rhythm he could not hear. The way her arm reached around to let her onyx hair down, the way she shook her head as almost in slow motion to let her hair bounce about her. Her body, with the dress that was so tight it was like skin, but not one of those cheap pleather dresses. It was finely made and tailored for her. Someone had spent a lot of time perfecting this dress for her. The way her fishnets didn't give off a 'lady of the night' vibe as they reached her heels, which seemed to be beating in the same rhythm as her eye lashes.

Attractive?

"I find you amazing," Rich muttered as he finished half the drink she gave him and almost spit it up. "What is this? It tastes like rotten licorice."

"Rotten?" Mia looked amused at him as she drank the same green drink she gave him. "It's absinthe. One might say the drink of the gods. Back in the 1900s, artists and poets drank this to excess, believing that their art excelled from it. It actually originated in the 18th century in Switzerland. They sell fake versions of it here in this country, but if you go to the right bars in the right places, you can get yourself a bottle of the real stuff."

"And this is…"

"The real stuff."

Rich's iWatch went off. Didn't he turn it off? He had seventeen missed calls and an endless amount of text messages.

"I'm sorry," Rich went to turn off it off, but it wouldn't turn off. "It's work stuff. This is rude of me. My focus should be on you."

"Your focus should be where you want it to be." Mia was eyeing him over as he tried to turn his phone and iWatch off. "Those things never made sense to me. You have a phone that already can give you a vast amount of information, and on that phone is a clock. What is the point of having both? It seems redundant in my mind. Technology will be the end of us all. The more electricity that is in the air, and the more fuzz that's around blocks the above."

"The above?" Rich was confused as he frantically was trying to make his phone stop going off and turn his iWatch off. "I don't know what's wrong with this thing or why work wants me so late at night. I know this is rude, but being the boss of your own company isn't an easy task. I'll make sure my assistant stops texting me. My focus is on you, Mia."

"Not your wife?" Mia's leg brushed up against Rich once more as his phone began to actually ring in his pocket. How did it get turned from vibrate to ring? "How many times has Amanda called and texted you now?"

It was close to two in the morning. He must have gotten too drunk and told her all of this. Beer, liquor, a pill, absinthe. Maybe he was missing a part of this night where he confessed.

But... something... something wasn't right...

"You don't care that I have a wife?" Rich was trying to search his memory for a conversation with Mia about his wife, Amanda. "I was at the bar tonight. I just thought I'd make friends. I came alone and thought making friends wouldn't hurt anyone. I could use a friend or two."

"I thought you had plenty of friends." Mia's smile never faltered. "I thought you were about to call one right before I introduced myself to you."

His phone rang as loud as it could in his pocket, and his iWatch was streaming text messages from his wife, Amanda. Literally all of them at once, a glitch, just streaming down his iWatch. They just wouldn't stop, and they all said similar things…

"Where are you?" Mia read one of the text messages out loud without even looking down at his watch. "Why aren't you home? Are you ok? Hunny? Love? Did you get into an accident? Should I call someone? I'm worried? Where are you?"

As Mia spoke the text messages, each one sprawled out on his iWatch. Each one was directly on point, each one directly exact to what she was saying.

Rich looked at Mia in terror.

"I think it's best I get home. This wasn't a good idea." Rich began to put his coat on inside out and was too drunk and too high, but he could still… lie. "I've never cheated on her before. I love my wife. Today was just a bad day. I came to the bar alone, and after a couple of drinks, I wound up talking to you. You are a seducer. A seductress. An enchantress. Probably can afford all of this from being a whore. I wonder how much you were planning on charging me tonight."

Mia shrugged, took a sip of her drink, and waved at him to go away.

Rich wrapped his scarf around his neck as he stumbled toward the front door. It was locked. From the inside.

Rich stood there for an eternity. His phone still going off in his pocket, his iWatch still buzzing, with Mia still chirping from the background.

"Rich, please answer me. Rich, please call me back. Rich, please…" Then Mia's voice dropped a few octaves.

Then bump by bump, hair by hair, was raised all across Rich's body as her voice became not of this world. The entire energy in the room shifted, as in the shadows, he saw her remove her dress. The entire feeling of the air around him was turning, "Please Rich. Not again."

Rich turned to look at the couch, but then the lights flickered off. The sounds he heard next were ones you could never forget. Cracking bones, ripping skin, as if someone had popped and cracked each and every bone in their body. In the shadows, he watched Mia rise ten or more feet into the air. He saw long twisted horns grow out of her head, skeletal bat-like wings spread out from her back. Glowing slits of glowing blue eyes were staring at him. Mia... it? It let out a slight roar, and as Rich saw its mouth drop a foot and expose rows upon rows of fangs, he began to run.

Like the fool he was, he ran upstairs, Maybe this wasn't her... it's house. Maybe someone else was home. He pulled his phone out of his pocket to dial 911, but all that was on his screen were his wife's frantic text messages. One after another, not even from tonight, but from the other nights as well and all the other times.

Rich, are you ok?

Rich, where are you?

Rich, why aren't you answering me?

Rich, are you ok?

Rich, please come home.

Rich, please answer me.

Rich, please.

"Rich," the deep and guttural voice called after him as he heard... heels? Coming towards him. Heavy on the ground and widened, as it had grown immensely, "Please. Answer me. Rich. Please. Are you ok? Rich, please come home."

Fee-Fi-Fo-Fom.

He began knocking on door after door, all of them locked from the outside. He had covered the first level as the monster began to make its way up the stairs. He fell as he slipped on the rug on the floor, banging on each door. Slowly, pounding each step as it lurched its way up, he caught a glimpse of a female body with nude dark yellow skin, a giant with twisted horns, crooked wings, and arms that expanded with long nails… no claws… those were claws.

Lights please stay out, Rich thought. *This is just a combination of absinthe and drugs and liquor. This is all a bad dream. I need to find a bed, and I can sleep.*

Rich tore up another flight of stairs as the monster let out another guttural noise. He stumbled over his feet and tossed his jacket back at it. He heard his jacket being caught by the monster, and it ripped it in shreds within a second.

This is only a dream.

You are asleep next to Amanda.

You are home in your house.

Your golden retriever is at your feet.

You will wake up soon.

"Foolish mortal," the guttural rasps were about him, "this is your reality now."

Rich was on the top floor of the expensive brownstone. All the doors had no light coming from under them, except one, all the way at the end of the hallway. A set of double doors. The monster's weight was taking its time to climb each and every step. A terrible sound echoed as Rich felt a set of adrenaline catch him as he sprinted down the hallway. He could have sworn he heard someone begging for help from one of the rooms. He pushed open the double doors at the end of the hallway...

It was a master bedroom decorated in the most elegant of modern fashions. The plush carpet sunk under his feet, and the white with the golden lined drapes hit the floor. The bed was perfectly made, white linens with golden accents. A mirror was on the wall and a large walk in closet was filled with similar dresses like Mia had worn that evening, an entire section just for shoes and purses. The bathroom was large, complete with a glass door shower and claw foot tub. This could have been featured in a high-class magazine for some impressive executive or famous celebrity. This wasn't just rich money. This was the money of someone who owned his or her own planes and boats. This wasn't the home of a creature.

It's just the combination of toxins, Rich tried to relax himself. *I just need to sleep this off.*

But the pounding of footsteps was coming. Slowly. Down the hall. In no rush. Rich felt like he was going to have a heart attack. This is real. This is happening. I need to get out of here. I can't just sleep this off.

There was a balcony. He quickly went and opened the doors. The snow was gusting about him as he stepped out onto the balcony. He looked at his iWatch and another text from his wife, Amanda, came in,

Who is Mia?

What the hell was going on, Rich thought. *What the hell is happening?*

Rich stood at the balcony for a second, looking down. If he would jump, he would be dead. So what, passed through his mind. So fucking what. He lived a life of…

Claws grabbed his back as he was flung onto the bed. Out of the long mouth were long fangs as from the back of it's mouth sludge exploded at each of his hands and feet, which stuck him to the bed. In front of him stood a creature. It was still Mia… but her blue eyes had grown into terrible looking glowing blue orbs that were slits. Long skeletal wings sprouted from her back and were lifting and lowering with each breath she took. Her blue lips had elongated and extended downward exposing rows and rows of sharp teeth. Her face had sunken in, and her skin was the darkest yellow he had ever seen, lined with purple veins that he could actually see dark murky substances pulse through them. Her hair was messed around two horns that gnarled their way out of her head and pointed to sharp tips at the top. But her body… her body was still fantastic… Her bosoms had grown, and her figure was still perfective but just massive in size. She somehow still had heels on and was thumping her way around the bed.

"Let me finish that thought for you," Mia said. "You have lived a lie. You have always lived a lie. You convinced your cousin as kids that what you two were doing together was ok. Actually violating him with your hands and body and mouth, lying to him for your own enjoyment. Now he

suffers from addiction issues that are on you. You still
fantasize about it as you touch yourself. Which you do a lot,
don't you? You married Amanda, a girl you've known for
more than half your life. You had girlfriends in college
while she was off studying elsewhere. Girls dumb enough to
believe that one day you'd leave her for them. You wear
sunglasses and a hat when you first meet guys because you
are scared they will know who you are, but you have been
touched by as many guys as you have girls. Rot. Scum.
Despicable. This wasn't your first time staying late at a bar
in hopes of finding something to enter, something to
destroy, something else to place your hands on. You have
done this time and time before. You have a boyfriend who
you make promises to. You tell him you'll buy him presents
and take him on trips. A mistress who you actually take on
trips and spend nights with in the city. Guys from your
improv class who you take into bathrooms and slide your
small and unimpressive member into. Hand jobs from
people you work with, interns who you touch in promises of
getting them actual jobs. You spend your days cruising
craigslist for both men and women. But what sickens me
the most? What made me smell you from miles upon miles
away? Your lack of empathy. Your lack of care. Your lack
of self-awareness for what you are doing to these people.
The selfishness that rises off you is of that which I've never
experienced. Richard, you fit the bill, and I must feed to
remain on this realm. I was young once, long before your
civilization and long before that. A time where magic was a
norm and creatures roamed freely. A time before dinosaurs
and before that. As we've begun to call it, a time before

written history. I used to eat what I could. I used to munch down… but somewhere along the way, I developed a conscious. I developed a sense of care for… humans. I couldn't just feed like I used to. I couldn't just eat them down. I developed a mental rule book as I began to know compassion and actual care. A code that has kept me from not being hungry for all the years I have been alive. A number you couldn't even conceive in your head. I only feed on those who left to their own lives would just continue to hurt people with cruelty. Tell me, Rich, do you believe in cruelty?"

Rich stared at the ten-foot beast of a woman that was towering over him and the bed. Even in her horror, she was a fantastic creature to look at. Could they join forces? Could he ride her back and her wings? Could he convince her to eat his wife and she teach him how to live for…

"No," Mia shook her large head. "No. I was born this way. I was created this way. This has been me since I was born… You."

She lifted a clawed finger, about a foot long towards him, as the sludge began to harden him in place.

"You have made choices." All ten feet of her spread her legs as she climbed on top of him, just over him. He couldn't have had sex with her if he wanted to. He was too drunk to even get it up, and she was… enormous… every part of her. Nor was his member that impressive. "You have decided and chosen to be this selfish king baby. You have blinded your wife with lies and a smile. You have blinded all around you with this victim act, like you are some sad boy at a bar who can't get any attention. I bet you were attractive once. I bet years back I would be looking at a stallion of a man someone who any girl or boy would fall victim to. But the lies catch up with you, don't they? Amanda finds things. Your parents see your pupils every day. Your cousin hates you more and more for the way you violated him as a kid. You know nothing of pain, as you are the one who causes it. You just don't care. You actually do not care. You are cruelty. You are what is wrong with this world."

Rich could feel the sludge tighten around his arms and legs. She spat one final time, and it wrapped his neck. The oozing, slithering, sludge, made up of what felt like the wettest worms wrapped around his neck tightened just enough that it wasn't strangling him, and it wasn't killing him. But at this moment he wanted to die. This… Mia held up a mirror to him, and he saw his life. He just wanted to die.

"Kill me then," Rich let out pathetically. "Just… just kill me."

"Kill you?" Mia let out a roar of laughter in her true form, still straddling him, "Do you know how many bedrooms are in this brownstone? How many places like this I have around the world? They are filled with clones of you. Men who cheat and lie. Men who rape and destroy. Men who touch children or their cousins and siblings. Men who think it's ok to whip out their penis… in your case… however small - and do as they please upon the world. I never asked to be born into what I am…"

"What the fuck are you?"

"The Japanese call me a Yuki-Onna, a snow woman, a snow queen, a snow witch... but South Park did a pretty good job portraying my kind, as I can survive summers. I am a Succubus." Mia's gigantic yellow head with the purple veins and long jaws and jagged rows of teeth bent down low, and a long slivering tongue a yard long licked Rich across his face, which felt like wet leather. "I need to feed on men to survive. But. Over the years, my heart... or whatever is in my chest... has grown warm and caring. I don't just kill like I did when I was young. I pick. I choose. I hunt. You won't die, Rich. You won't die for a long, long time, I'll keep you alive as long as I can as I feed on various parts of you. I will divulge myself and then let you refresh so I can divulge again. Your lifetime is a speck on my timeline, but I will make sure you suffer. Just as those who have suffered before you. Just as you have made so many suffer with your lies and cruelty."

"You... you're... you are a..."

"No, Rich. You are the monster."

Mia cracked her head back and sunk her teeth into Rich's stomach.

Somewhere in New Jersey, in a quiet neighborhood where kids still go trick or treating and nice houses line blocks filled with happy families, a house stood, a nice home, that Rich hadn't bought himself as all the money he ever had had come from his parents. In a living room with a fireplace sat his wife.

More annoyed than worried, more angry than in care. Amanda knew. She had always known. As her phone gave her an electric shock and her golden retriever jumped, she stumbled out of the chair she was curled up on and put her back against a door. The dog whimpered at her phone which just sizzled and sparkled.

Her wedding ring shocked her finger, and she tossed it off. As she watched it roll away on the wooden floor of their home in a quiet suburbia town, it melted. She watched her diamond and silver around it just melt away, as if it was ice cream.

Amanda crossed the room and bent low to look at it. A diamond was melting before her eyes, a promise that was made years ago dissipating as the ring just left a small burn mark on the floor. It was all ash and dust. She blew at it, and it scattered away. She took a sponge and with a couple of scrapes, any sign of it was gone.

This feeling overcame her. Something new and original. Something she couldn't explain because she knew nothing else for the past sixteen years.

Weights were being lifted off her shoulders. A sensation she could never explain, a phenomena she could never know. Until Rich didn't return that night, until he didn't come home the next day, when he didn't show up for work, when he didn't call or check in with anyone.

A search for him began. Flyers. Tv ads. His parents cried desperately for him to return on national news. Tv ads. Flyers. Searches for him. Tv ads. Flyers…

But.

Amanda felt free.

Student of the Year

Autumn 2016

"Three more rounds, loser." Kevin hit the controller again, losing for the fifteenth time. "I'm not tired. It's not that late."

"Man," Brad was up and hopping in his bed on the other side of the dorm room, "I have mid-terms I actually studied for. I have a game tomorrow I am actually going to play in. I have…"

"I get it, jerk. Shut up."

Awkward silence.

"Kevin," Brad sat up in his bed before tossing off his hoodie, not an ounce of fat on him. "I could take you running. We could workout in private. Go for a hike. I'm sure your grandmother must know some nice hikes around here. Just come walking around campus a few times with me, man. I could introduce you to people. Who knows what could happen? You'd feel better about yourself. You'd be able to leave the room more often, maybe give the pizza joint a break from coming here three times a day. Come on, man. What do you say?"

"Night faggot."

"I don't know why I bother. Take a fucking shower. I almost vomited walking in here earlier." Brad had tried everything to get Kevin to stop being such a glutton, and it irritated him. How could someone just not care about themselves at all? "I'll report you to the Dean if you don't, and that'd be more embarrassing for you than other students. She, I know, will make you shower."

Brad put his head to his pillow as Kevin let out a huge fart, on purpose, before going back to a different game on his computer. Their tiny dorm room seemed even tinier. The smell of his roommate made Brad cough, and it namaste'd that anger right out of him.

Kevin and Brad were the worst roommates paired together in college history.

Freshman roommates were never a joy or pleasure, but this was some cosmic joke. Kevin was pushing 230, sat at his computer when he wasn't in basic liberal arts classes, and played video games online all day. He spent all of his money on pizza and messy chips. He smelled, didn't change his clothes and would pocket food from the cafeteria. He had no major in mind, but he did decide on being a wizard this time around on his online game. That was the biggest decision of his week besides trying triple crust pizza stuffed with bacon and cheese.

Brad walked into a room, smiled, and everyone else smiled. He had been a model as a kid, did some commercials, and then made the move into sports. With a full scholarship and long distance relationship with his high school sweetheart who he was going to marry, no matter how many sorority girls threw themselves at him, he prided himself on being faithful. He wore the ring he was going to give her around his neck at all times. He studied advanced classes, was going to med school, and would be a doctor. He had a picket white fence and a house on a street called Sun Drop Court all planned out in his mind.

"I need some air from you, man." Brad hopped down and out of bed, "I am going to take a shower. Then you are. Got it?"

"You can't make me shower, frat boy faggot, gay little stupid…"

Brad had Kevin on the floor so fast with his arm at his neck. It didn't matter if someone was a hundred or three hundred pounds. With his background in martial arts and years of sports, Brad would be able to get them on the floor.

"Drop that ugly word from your mouth. Do you know people around here are calling you Shrek? It's been three weeks of this shit. I am going to shower. When I get back, all this trash will be cleaned up, and you are going to take a shower." Brad pushed his arm deeper into Kevin's flabby neck. Brad was all muscle, and Kevin broke under it. "Say it. Or I swear… You want to see classic frat boy moves? I'll get my football pals up here. You got to make me threaten you about taking a damn shower? About hitting the gym with me once in a while? Just give me a chance man."

"Fine."

"Good! Christ!" Brad tossed his clothes off, and Kevin quickly looked away. Brad's side of the room was perfectly organized. Towels folded, clothes hung up by color and collar versus V-neck order, and shoes in a row. Nothing was on his desk, and his books were tucked neatly in drawers. Kevin's side was just all of these things tossed together: food and books mixed with socks and old half eaten hot pockets. "Just try Kevin. That's all I'm asking of you man. Just try. A few workouts, a few days spent hiking, and you'll just feel better. I promise."

"Fine."

"I'm going to shower." Brad wrapped a recently washed towel around his waist, "When I get back...?"

"I get it." Kevin had his head down, dug out a garbage bag, and began to toss all of his trash away. Brad had met Kevin's parents and got that 'yah we used to beat our kid so what' vibe. He had done nothing but try to break through to him in the past three weeks.

A shower. That was a start.

Poor kid, Brad thought, *we can't control where we come from, but we can control where we go.*

It was after two in the morning, and the hallways of the dorm were completely empty. A light flickered overhead as the heater coughed against the wall. With his soap in hand, Brad made his way down the hallway where the showers were located. It was eerily quiet, each step knocking around and echoing over itself. These buildings were old, so the floors creaked and the doors squealed when you opened them.

Overhead another light flickered, and Brad made the turn and pushed the bathroom door open. The lights in the bathroom were off. Weird. He switched them on, and for a second, nothing happened. One by one, then, each light popped on. Brad took a look at himself in the mirror and smiled because he planned on always looking this good, always taking care of himself, and always doing right by others and helping those in need.

He went into the showers, leaving his towel behind. He pushed through the plastic dividers and went to the biggest shower space in the back, the one everyone always wanted. He turned the nozzle, and with a couple of coughs that echoed throughout the pipes, water began to spit out. It was cold as ice at first, but after a moment or two, it got to the right temperature.

He began to hum some old Counting Crows song as he washed himself. Moments were rare that the bathroom was empty, let alone no one else in the showers. The small secret pleasures of the college life. Suddenly the plastic shifted.

"Hey?"

No answer. Another shower turned on. It was hard to see through the fog, but a shadow was there.

"Late night shower, eh?"

Another shower turned on, and then the next, and then the next. All twelve shower heads were spewing burning hot water as the dark figure seemingly floated slowly from one side to the next. Brad's skin began to crawl, and his tightened up as he prepared to fight.

"Hey." The lights above began to flicker off. "This isn't funny."

Through the plastic dividers in a fast motion, he was tossed like a bean bag out of the shower area and into the bathroom.

A large hand grabbed Brad and lifted him into the air with ease. Easily standing over six and a half feet, it flipped him across the bathroom. Brad got up and went to run into it because he was after all an athlete; he had to have some leverage.

But, he smashed into what felt like a wall of bricks. A solid entity with no bounce or flab or skin. Just solid, like stone. Brad scrambled. Falling back and hazy, it brought down a giant machete into him.

He caught a flash of its face, and he tried to yell for help.

It took the machete high and swung it down again into Brad's throat.

Over and over and over again, the floors were now covered in pieces of Brad. The only sound in the bathroom was the melody of the many places Brad's blood was bleeding in drops, a song of horror dripping onto the floor.

The lights flickered out, but when they flickered on... written on the mirror... in Brad's blood was A+.

- -

Kevin was the one who found him. He went to the bathroom to get more trash bags, as he had been throwing away all the garbage from his side of the room. Brad had broken through to him that night, and that alone hurt him deeper than he thought it would.

Dean Lorena Schatten had decided to keep this on a need to know basis with the family and campus security, but of course she couldn't keep it completely quiet. Word had spread and had spread quickly over the internet and onto many social networks.

Brad was prom king at his high-school, and his smile could be spread across billboards. A boy not even twenty losing his life? That covered everyone's newsfeed.

That's how TJ found out about the 'Monster at Prescott,' Prescott being one of the country's top Ivy League schools. He was currently sitting on a bench outside Asbury Hall waiting for Kevin to emerge. He had seen a picture of the kid and had checked out his Facebook profile. Kevin Morehead was certainly not the pride of the family. Being that big must be a struggle in life. The poor kid must have had a hard time in high school living up to his family's reputation. From what he gathered from Facebook, Kevin grew up in a large house on a lake with boats, but one would never assume this from the way he presented himself. That was enough pressure on the kid… and then having a golden jock as a roommate? Kevin could have very well killed him, but TJ doubted it the minute he saw Kevin leave Asbury, his head down, shuffling his feet.

"Hey man! Kevin!" TJ still looked like he belonged in college and quickly caught up with Kevin. "How you holding up?"

"Coming to make fun of me? Blame me for killing Brad?" Kevin shot TJ a sad look. No doubt he had been tormented after this as well. TJ could tell this was a kid who not only got beaten up in school, but his home life must have been rough. He reeked. TJ couldn't tell the last time Kevin showered… it was awful. Could he not smell himself?

"You just lost your roommate, man. Only cruel people would make fun of you, and for something like that?

They have karma coming." TJ put an arm around Kevin, as much as possible, and withstood the odor from him. "Kevin, he got slashed to pieces by a machete. You couldn't have done anything to save him. Ignore idiots. They'll find someone else to make fun of soon enough."

"Thanks." Kevin shot TJ a look of confusion as kindness wasn't a norm in his life. "No one has been this nice to me ever like Brad. I was nothing but mean to him, obvious jealously. You couldn't even hate how perfect the kid was cause he was so nice. But I was so angry inside, and so... I struggled just to get up every day, and I spend my days in fantasy lands on computers because I thought the world wouldn't want someone like me in it. That night Brad broke through to me. He wanted to help me lose weight. Help me clean up. Help me eat better and go hiking. No one has ever given two shits about me. Now he's gone. No one has been that nice to me ever."

"People make fun of other people because they have hate inside of them, Kevin. Why not remember Brad by following through with his advice? I saw someone post online that the kid shit gold and positivity. Workout, eat better, get out more... Not everything is awful. Any of us can shit gold and positivity if we put our minds to it, so just work for it. The world is not a bad place."

"Yes it is." Kevin gave TJ a look that made him shiver. "I saw a large shadow. Almost seven feet and wide. It was standing at our door before it vanished. I thought I was seeing things. I play a lot of video games, watch a lot of movies, and don't get out much. I've seen random stuff before, but this gave me the chills to the bone. At that

157

moment, I knew Brad had been killed. Whatever it was, though, it wasn't human."

Kevin hurried off without another word, and a bunch of sorority girls huffed as they passed by him. Lots of pink was heading TJ's way through the stone ivy covered buildings, and they smiled the minute they saw him.

"Hi. You're coming to a party tonight. I'm Clarissa," the hot blonde said. She was wearing a pink tube top, pink skirt, pink Uggs, and a pink and gold sorority pin near her cleavage. The other was a black girl, just as hot and just as pink. She winked at him. "I'll learn your name tonight, big shot. I'm a cheerleader, one of the top in the nation. Maybe I'll show you just how flexible I am."

"It's true," the other girl smiled and winked. "You should cum play later."

The word 'cum' emphasized heavily.

They laughed as they bounced off. Oh, to be back in college.

"Trust me, I'll be there."

"I came." He smiled, finding himself at a big college party. Black lights, painted skin, large pitchers of punch and jello shots. In another world, he'd enjoy this for what it was: a college orgy. "Being a freshman here so far is awesome, and this is just the cherry on some cake. I've heard this was a party school and that Kappa's epic parties were not to be missed."

"Especially when you are this attractive! You

probably get invited to lots of VIP places," Clarissa, one of the head sorority sisters of Kappa, said smiling. How could she still be standing after six jello shots in a row? "I mean, let me get you a jello shot. They taste like truffles. Chivalry can work on both ends, right? Maybe later I'll be holding a door open for you."

Innuendoes.

"Thanks," TJ let on a smile that along with his other features had made his job easier. "I'll be right here."

TJ scanned the room. This was some sorority house. The ceilings climbed to the second level where a finely shined balcony wrapped around to a grand staircase that led down and onto the first floor. A chandelier that he doubted was crystal, but with the money these girls' daddies had? Nah, it was a fine crystal chandelier. He was surprised they didn't have all the fine white leather furniture covered for the parties, but his grandmother never bothered to cover furniture when her drunken friends stumbled about at her grand parties. Same concept, because old women knew how to party just as well as these girls.

The entire campus goes to parties like this; you don't just miss them. If he was going to get any leads on why Brad the golden retriever got hacked into dog meat, he figured why not start here? Plus...

"Are you going to rush a house?" Clarissa was back, a typical sorority girl with her hair up in a ponytail. Makeup. Short skirt. Tight sparkly top... way too tight of a top. Tiffany jewelry decorated every inch of her. "For a freshman, you are quite the man. I don't normally flirt below my grade level, but look at you."

"Hit puberty early I guess. Greek life doesn't seem like the road for me," he growled jokingly. "I'm more of a lone wolf."

Clarissa was up against him with her drink, brushing the right areas. Uh-oh… TJ needed to think of Jabba the Hut naked on a cold day… no, Bruce Jenner naked on a cold day… no, Anthony Hopkins dancing naked on a cold day. There that worked.

"Well, maybe I can show you a thing or two about Greek life you might enjoy."

They danced together, and she smelled like fresh candy. He rubbed his head against hers, and even found her lips on his neck. TJ actually closed his eyes for a second until a voice in his subconscious yelled at him. Dude, you don't even go to this school. TJ flashed his eyes around the room trying to return to why he drove so far to get here. Besides the typical college antics taking place around him, something else caught his eye. Across the walls were a ton of awards, medals, and honors.

"Seems like you ladies do a lot of good work."

Clarissa came in close to TJ's ear, licked it, and then bit on it just enough that all of his thoughts of naked things on cold days ended. She laughed, playfully.

"Those are mostly mine," Clarissa pushed him off just enough while batting her blue eyes. "I'm president of this here establishment. I'm a senior, robbing the cradle with you, I know. Who can explain attraction, or why would you even want to explain it? I helped raise money to build this house, and most of the girls did a lot of the heavy lifting. Every dollar you paid at that door goes to charity. I turned what was known as a party brothel of sluts into a charitable house known for giving and excelling in academics. While Dean Schatten still thinks we are running a secret coke distribution place here, we aren't your TV sorority. Big companies are noticing us. I've got an offer after Prescott that would blow your mind."

"Very impressive." Just like Brad, a modest overachiever. Yet she stretched the word blow out too long, and TJ felt like Clarissa had an area of the sorority house she would want to show him later. Her bed. "Did you know Brad?"

"That poor Ken doll that got sliced up? No, it's only been three weeks since school started back up, and he was only a freshman, but I heard…"

The doors of the sorority house were kicked opened, and flashlights began to shine everywhere. In the shadows, two very tall figures accompanied by a smaller one took the scene. Kids began to scramble and run out the back door.

"That's enough, ladies," a strong female voice snapped into the darkness. The lights all flashed on at once, and everyone made noises. "Another drunken night at the Kappa house. I will shut you down, Clarissa."

Standing in between two large security guards, holding her cane out at Clarissa like the Wicked Witch held her finger to Dorothy, was who he assumed was the Dean of the college. TJ had done some reading up on her: Dean Lorena Schatten.

"There isn't a single drop of booze anywhere here," Clarissa responded. TJ looked down at the jello shot he hadn't taken and smelled it. Clarissa was right. It was all Perrier and fruit punch, and the jello shots were just creative mixtures of jello. "Search the place."

TJ eyed Dean Schatten annoyed that she was interrupting his break from his hunt, which was supposed to land him in Clarissa's room. He automatically didn't like her, but he felt like that was the norm. Slowly making her way in on a cane, the Dean was slightly hunched over with short and choppy black hair covering her head. She glared down at all of the students with displeasure. Her shadow lined eyes flashed around the room studying and remembering each face, and then her eyes fell on TJ. She sneered at him.

"Kiss me," he said to Clarissa, and he grabbed her in for a kiss. He didn't like the look the Dean had given him, almost as if she knew he wasn't a student. He kissed the beautiful sorority girl until he felt the eyes off of him.

"Well... a lone wolf who knows what he wants. Growl." Clarissa looked pleased for a second, then remembered the Dean was there. "I gotta go... for now... find me later."

Sadly he couldn't promise that.

Clarissa and the stunning black girl from earlier went up to the Dean. They must be the two leaders here.

"It's the beginning of a new semester! How else are we supposed to meet all of the new students?"

"Enough!" Dean Schatten snapped at Clarissa and then sneered at her. The old woman's contorted face slowly looked them over with utter distaste. "You smell like a brothel. Sex, drugs, and rock and roll... not under my watch! Search the entire place. Search it! I'll bet they have drugs in their rooms. You'll regret this, my pretty and all your sorority girls, too!"

"You heard the Dean! Search the place," one of the security guards barked. These weren't normal campus security guards, the ones you could convince to smoke a joint with you out back. These... they had guns. "Start with the girls' rooms upstairs."

"This has gotten ridiculous," Clarissa threw her hands up as she and two of her sisters made their way up the stairs to allow campus security into their rooms. "Find someone else to bother."

TJ took that moment to slip out the back door. He could see as he was exiting that the Dean was searching the room, like the wicked witch had risen to question all about her sister, hating to make assumptions, to look for him.

He almost expected to hear, 'Who killed my sister? Who killed the witch of the east? Was it you?' with her fingers pointed at him.

Dean Lorena Schatten, burrrrr.

Across campus was a gymnasium that was going to be redone next summer with a healthy grant the school had received from a common donor. An athlete was taking advantage of having the entire place to himself.

Joe Kuder was the best swimmer on the swim team.

Not a cocky notion or an over exaggerated fact, he was the best. His fraternity was known for having straight

A's, and if you got a certain GPA, you could try out for the swim team or any other team. It was an honor, truly. Joe had perfect grades, and there were talks of him heading to the Olympics. However, he kept his mind steady and focused to not to get ahead of himself. It was also a rite of passage to be part of the swim team in his fraternity. His friends joked that at the Olympics he'd stand out and be easy to find because he was a ginger with fire red hair. But, he was used to the ginger jokes after all of those South Park episodes.

He had skipped the sorority party tonight to come to the gymnasium. The hot art teacher was jogging above, and he had the pool all to himself. Literally heaven, a total orgasm... not the hot art teacher but having the lanes all to himself.

Certain things make different people happy. Some people enjoy rolling around with a puppy, others enjoy cooking, and some enjoy spending their afternoons playing video games and smoking joints on campus. There are certain moments of bliss that you can lose yourself in and just enjoy the moments of life that aren't so bad.

Joe lived for these moments. He waited until the teacher left and put his iPod on the small speakers he brought with him. Eminem came on with the song that sounded like he was saying spaghetti over and over again. Joe took off his gym shorts and shirt.

Every year he asked his parents to put a lap pool in their backyard. He had a feeling that if he kept his GPA where it was at, he'd see that pool and be able to act like a child getting their new puppy on Christmas morning. Only time would tell.

His family couldn't have been more proud of him. Not only was he the best swimmer on the team, he was on the short list for the highest honor you could receive at Prescott.

TJ was at the back of the sorority house, and he immediately began to inhale cigarette and weed smoke thanks to a group standing close by smoking both cigarettes and marijuana.

"What?" the prettiest of the bunch said, startled by how quickly he came out of the back door. "Who the hell are you?"

"I'm TJ," he smiled, but none of the half dozen kids smiled back. "Freshman here."

"Fresh meat," a boy said from the back. "Let's tie him to a tree, cover him in honey, and see if a bear comes. Pass that joint. It's the last of that Heller Kush, and you don't find nugs like that out here."

Yah, let's see you try that. TJ could handle a bunch of potheads.

"I'm Dani," the pretty brunette said between puffs of cigarette smoke. She was obviously the leader of the pack. They were all dressed in dark colors, campus hoodies, and tattered jeans. Something told TJ they weren't invited to the sorority party, so they were standing at the back of the house smoking in protest. "Ignore them, we've had enough fun with freshman for the night anyway. Plus after that blonde kid got hacked up like lunch meat, I wouldn't leave anyone tied to a tree… at least anyone that I liked. Do I like you, TJ?"

"I know where to score some awesome Heller Kush," TJ quickly replied, but he never did drugs in his life. Never planned on it nor knew where to 'score,' but every group had a key to entry, and…

"Ok," the kid who had threatened him before, who in no way would have been able to tangle him to a tree responded, "we like him."

"So you heard about that kid? Did any of you know him?"

"He was in my advanced math class, which for a freshman is impressive." Dani had finished one cigarette, crushed it under her hooker boot, and already had another in her mouth. "He sat next to me. I looked over, and he knew every answer and only raised his hand a couple of times during class. He couldn't have cut it in my higher math classes, but it was impressive for a freshman to be in advanced trig. Kid knew he was smart and didn't show it off, but he wasn't the type to let anyone copy his homework... no matter what they offered him."

Sex.

The gymnasium was as old as the school was and still had that 1950s vibe to it, which was the year it was erected. The crank that was used to roll and unroll the blue heavy covering for the pool was ancient. It normally took three guys to make it move easily. As Joe was on the smaller side, it took him a good five minutes to roll it half-way across the pool, which would leave two lanes open.

Joe headed over to his iPod and switched songs as a cold sensation passed through him. Eerily, Joe shuddered slightly, trying to shake that feeling of uncomfortableness away. For a second, a voice in his head told him to go to the sorority party, but he shook it off, for it was the voices of his frat brothers in his head. He knew he was going to get shit later for missing it. Clarissa and Melody would have noticed he wasn't there, and he'd get a lecture from Clarissa on how Greek life needs to stand together before the Dean takes them down.

Dean Schatten hated Greek life. She hated the parties, the drugs, and the booze. Kappa house was a dry house, though, and she never found as much as a fragment of weed there. Joe's Alpha house on the other hand, well, the Dean hadn't removed the ceiling boards yet, and if she did, she would be showered in various bags of weed and other fun party activities.

It's not that hard to outsmart a woman who is going on a thousand years old.

Joe stretched himself out, and for a second, he felt a breath on his neck that made him jump and scramble on the floor.

Old building, Joe thought. *Old buildings do creepy things on their own.*

He went over to the diving block, got into form, and dove in.

"You know we are on the pathway to becoming the number one school in the world?" said a random kid who was so stoned his eyes were basically shut. "We have a few students here, athletes, overachievers, and scholars, who are putting us on the map. That Brad kid, I heard about him before he even got here. He alone could have bumped this place up a notch."

These kids didn't seem like Prescott school material, none of them.

"Why don't you... I mean... If you don't... Why did you guys choose to come here?"

"Rude!" one of the girls next to Dani blurted out, her hoodie over her head. "Not buying the book because of the cover? All the Bible says is 'Holy Bible' across it on a dark leather cover, yet it's the number one selling book in the world. Has no cover, just a blank..."

"Allison, shut up. We don't look like the Ivy League type, right?" Dani smiled, a beautiful smile. But no they didn't, especially her. Dressed in a tight black dress, spiderweb fishnets, boots that went to her knees, and dark makeup. "I'm actually number one in the country in... I swear to God if any of you begin the jokes again, I will tie you to trees myself... in math. I've won various accolades and got a full ride here on it. Almost everyone on campus specializes in something..."

"But only a few are aces. That Brad kid was a star quarterback with a perfect GPA. Clarissa, the queen of

Kappa, has done more charity work and has turned that party house into a respectable place. Some Joe kid from Alpha house has the Olympics in his future for swimming, and some say he's going to be the next Michael Phelps." The guy who had threatened to tie him to a tree took a huge puff of his joint before continuing, but first went to pass the joint to TJ who shook his head - no need to start doing drugs now. "This entire campus is filled with kids with 'special abilities.' We are the closest to X-Men you will find. Hell, I bet if Dani focused enough she could levitate…"

"Ok. That's enough. You are stoned." Dani waved the puff cloud of marijuana out of her face. "What Tim means is, this college is filled with smarty smart pants. Gathered from all around the country, the few that are truly destined to greatness. Many CEOs, professional athletes, scientists who have found breakthroughs… You get the picture, but you would have known this if you actually went here. Are you a townie?"

"Yes." It'd be easier to explain being on a campus party living in town then why he was really here. He had a feeling he'd be fielded with roommate questions and focuses on majors. Plus Dani and Clarissa obviously didn't sit at lunch together, so he wouldn't have to worry about his stories getting muddled. "Just wanted to come check out what the fuss was about."

"Well," Dani smashed another cigarette under her heel, "the fuss is who gets named student of the year. Every year the Dean herself picks one student to be 'crowned' student of the year. At Prescott, that's like a key to any door you want, open up Narnia or… I'm getting a second hand high over here guys. You get it."

TJ thought he was beginning to get it.

"But this year Kevin Morehead is at the school," Dani rolled her eyes. "If I was the Dean, I'd be angry that my grandchild wasn't even in the running for student of the year."

"Wait… Brad's roommate? He's the Dean's grandson?"

"Yup," the boy with tying to tree threats blurted. "Mr. Starcraft got a full ride here, actually passed all the right tests and what not. If you are a Schatten, you attend Prescott school. His mother is a Schatten, though the last name Morehead must have added to his torture. But he doesn't specialize in anything except maybe a level six thousand wizard fag in world craft."

Dani's hand came around and smacked him. "What did we say about that word? It's like throwing the N word around, and you are smarter than that. Don't make yourself look dumb… dumber."

That was all TJ needed to hear. Now he needed to get back to his motel room he needed to tie all these pieces together.

"What?" Dani called after him playfully. "No kiss goodbye handsome?"

Joe ducked under the water, flipped himself around, and kicked back towards the other side. He had done his lap routine, and he had run through all the drills the coach would have had him do, including the out of pool warmups. He flashed an eye at the clock. How was it almost 2am already?

He looked around at the empty gymnasium, Eminem blurting out one of his 90s hits. Joe smiled and decided thirty minutes of free styling would be a nice way to finish the night. He began to slowly float backwards and then twisted under the water, swimming like a mermaid to the bottom. He came back up for a breath of air and decided to do the same in the deep end.

He took a big gulp of air and began to swim down as fast as he could to the deep end. He wouldn't have been able to hear the cranks turning, the blue pool covering moving at a fast pace across the open water. As he reached the top of the pool his head hit the blue covering, and he was pushed down.

Fluttering his legs, keeping himself afloat, he had just enough oxygen to breathe through the covering until a large hand grabbed him. The hand held his head underwater and then lifted it through the thick blue pool covering. It ducked him under again and held him there, long enough that he almost lost consciousness, which would have been a better fate.

The large hand circled around his entire head and tore him through the pool covering, pulling him up out of the pool with ease. Joe was tossed like a rag doll against the wall. A light flickered from above, wildly.

Joe went to get to his feet but slipped on the wet ground, and he heard something in his leg pop. He instantly let out a sound of pain, but the pain was gone the minute he saw what was coming towards him. It had to be at least seven feet tall and as wide as a linebacker. They were in darkness and he couldn't make out - it's? - features. It was coming at him and fast.

"Holy…" Joe scrambled to his feet and began to run, but somehow the beast of a creature was now in front of him. It was dressed in a tattered and torn uniform and even had a name tag on it that he couldn't make out, but its face.

A flicker of light on the gray skin, its missing eye, lips that were dripping away, and a toothless grin had been enough. He didn't need to see the full thing.

"Please, sir. Please. I was…" *I am now arguing with something that is not alive, this would make one hell of a scene of American Horror Story*, were Joe's final thoughts.

It lifted Joe over its head, and with one massive move ripped him in two, tossing the bottom half of him across the gymnasium like flicking a fly away. Joe's legs and bottom half smashed against the wall on the other side. It then ripped Joe's head off its torso and tossed the torso in the other direction. Finally, it crushed Joe's head between its massive hands and flung it towards the locker room - his ginger head rolling until it hit a wall.

As the light stopped flickering, it was gone. Eminem was still beating and echoing throughout the empty gym.

Across the floor written in Joe's blood: a crude drawing of an Olympic medal.

TJ was sitting in his motel room and had a picture of the Schatten family up on his computer. The picture had been taken at a recent family reunion at a gigantic estate on a hill. Whose? TJ couldn't decide. There had to be at least fifty of them in the picture. In the center was the Dean, sitting on a chair that was more throne like than anything else. On the ground next to her was a gaggle of children spread across the lawn in age order. Kevin was in the farthest corner of the picture, and he was so fat that half of his body was hidden behind one of the adults. He was looking away from the picture. Everyone else had smiles on their faces, except for the Dean; she was glaring at the camera with a look that made even TJ shudder.

Suspect one: Dean Schatten.

TJ pulled up all he could on her.

Lorena Schatten had been Dean of Prescott for 40 years, taking a 10 year leave to help bring order to an all girls school in Sweden back in 1998. Was known to have an iron fist, and was heavily involved in the progression of the school. She helped it climb to its Ivy League status. There were pictures of her shaking hands with presidents, various athletes, and CEOs who at one point came through her school. There was never a smile on her face, not even back in the late 70s when she was younger and less hag-like.

TJ hated to call them as he saw them because he had been wrong before, like when he threw holy water on a priest who he thought was a demon. Didn't realize el padre would have such a heavy hit to him.

This was kind of a touch and go thing for him at this point.

But, everything about Dean Schatten screamed witch.

Now her grandchild was on campus and wasn't in the running for student of the year. She was going to off every competitor he was up against first, but it looked like she had issues opening a jar. How could she murder a student? Was she summoning someone or something to do her dirty work? If so, who or what?

TJ would stop her.

"A meeting with Dean Schatten requires an appointment," a secretary who was as tightly wound as could be spat at him, looking him over. "She's a very busy woman and does not like being interrupted. Your name?"

TJ was in the Dean's grand office with red carpets, gold-dusted wallpaper, and pictures of various stone buildings on campus throughout the years. However, there were no couches or seats; there was nowhere for someone to wait for an appointment. Just a secretary's desk, a long hallway, and the two security guards from the night before stuck out. The ones with guns. They were guarding a double door that had Dean Lorena Schatten behind it.

"I'll call in for an appointment then," TJ smiled at the chunky unhappy looking middle aged secretary who just glared at him until he left. Well, that wasn't suspicious or weird. TJ was making his way out of the administration building when he saw a group of girls crying. One of them Clarissa. He stared over at her until she finally looked at him and just shook her head.

Dressed in the pink hoodie of her sorority, pink sweats, yoga pants and pink Uggs, she made her way over to him. Her blonde hair was pulled up on top of her head. She was still gorgeous, though - one of those girls who didn't need makeup to look pretty. Why do girls wear makeup anyway? Guys don't paint their faces, so why do girls? Focus TJ! ADD kicking in!

"What's wrong?" TJ asked as Clarissa threw her arms around him, pushing herself up against him. Oh no… cold places… naked Dean Schatten on a rainy day… "Are you ok?"

"Joe Kuder… an Alpha brother," Clarissa shook her head as Melody came over. "I can't even… Melody you tell him."

Clarissa buried her head into TJ's shoulder. This needed to stop… TJ hadn't had sex in forever. Literally, he was still a virgin. Sometimes just brushing up against him was enough to… Dean Schatten naked on a cold day, Dean Schatten naked on a cold day. Ok, all's good.

"He skipped our party," Melody said, almost as if it was a crime, "and went to the pool to practice. He's the best swimmer on our school's team. I heard rumors the Olympics were going to be in his future. They found him in three pieces, literally torn apart. Some crude blood drawing on the floor. It's all so terrible, I've never met a nicer kid."

"First Brad… Next Joe… Who's next?!" Clarissa was crying into TJ's shoulder, so he put an arm around her.

175

"You are so kind to comfort me. You make me feel safe. I just… Should we shut the school down? Should we petition? I mean whose going to be killed next?!"

"Probably you." He smelled the cigarette smoke before he saw Dani approach. "Brad, Joe, all student of the year nominees. I'm on that list…"

"Slut," Melody muttered and then raised her voice to speaking level. "Why would you be on that list?"

"Just because I don't play sorority doesn't mean I don't contribute to Prescott." Dani did an exaggerated bow, and the two cohorts she had with her laughed. "I am top in math here and in the country. Combine that with the hours of community service I put in and a book I wrote on bipolar disease about my mother who killed herself when I was sixteen, I'd say you and I are getting closer and closer to the top of that list."

So was Kevin Morehead-Schatten, TJ thought. If only he could get the Dean alone… TJ zoned out as the two girls argued with each other. If the Dean was summoning this thing to kill off overachievers, she had to be doing it from her office. Why else would she put two armed security guards outside those doors? She was an old woman and a paranoid one. Behind those doors her arthritis ridden hands could do whatever was needed to summon or conjure… Is that the same thing? Whatever. To bring forth whatever is killing these kids.

TJ had an idea and knew it was a dumb one.

"Clarissa," Melody put her hand out at Dani who was still trying to argue with her, "let's go. The riffraff isn't worth our time."

"You are so right. Especially after one of our school's best died." Clarissa kissed TJ on the cheek. "I'm going to see you later, right? Maybe one night this week we can catch a movie and cuddle back at my room."

"Oh for God's sake, and I'm the slut," Dani rolled her eyes and lit another cigarette. "Run off sorority wallpaper, run off."

TJ waited until Clarissa and Melody had vanished between a couple of the large stone buildings covered in ivy before turning his gaze back to Dani.

"What?" God, what is it with girls named Danielle and Jackie. They tend to be such bitches. "You forget something townie? Convince Clarissa the sorority queen to take you in. You've lost my small faith in humanity."

"I'm all out of Heller Kush, and I thought maybe one of your friends could help me score some weed." TJ kept his eyes steady on the two guys behind Dani who exchanged looks with her. She nodded, and then they shrugged and nodded back. "Hook a kid up?"

"Yah, man. Meet us in front of Asbury in an hour. How much?"

"Sixty dollars' worth." TJ had never bought weed, but he had apparently said the right thing because off they went.

"I'm going to take this opportunity to take a nap. My roommate will be in class for three hours, and I have to tutor all night." Dani flicked her cigarette into the bushes, looking at it as if she hoped they'd catch fire. She caught TJ's reaction. "Yes. I tutor. Yah know? It's taught to us when we are young, but we never listen. Everything isn't

177

always as it seems. I like dressing in tight dresses and dark makeup and fishnets. Who cares?"

"We certainly don't. Not us," the two guys behind her mumbled at the same time, and she laughed.

"If we were all blind, wouldn't it be so much better? We would actually have to rely on our intellect and senses. Not judging the outside before knowing what is in. The richest man in the world could be the unhappiest, the poorest could be the happiest, the most beautiful girl could have a heart of char, while a prom queen could be dying of depression inside. TJ, to grow is to know that what you see, isn't always what is. I never saw Melody wear pink till she joined Kappa. I've also had lunch with Kevin Morehead, and he has to be the nicest and loneliest kid I've ever met. If we lost our eyes, for a day, we would be a kinder race. Not those who see the Mercedes and assume everything is working under the hood."

TJ was left speechless as Dani picked up her dark purse and made her way across the other side of campus.

"Where is he?" one of Dani's dudes said to the other. "We said an hour."

"I give him five more minutes, and then we go light up ourselves… fuck."

The two security guards were coming at both at them at rapid speed, the two who were normally positioned outside of the Dean's office. They grabbed both kids and roughly had them in the grass in front of their dorm, missing the sidewalk by inches. These weren't just campus security guards; they were military trained. Dean Schatten didn't mess around.

"The marijuana, gentlemen?"

About an hour ago, the secretary's phone rang and gave an anonymous tip that some students were selling weed across campus in front of Asbury hall. The chunky secretary bumbled her way and knocked on the Dean's office.

"Yes."

Opening the door into a gilded decorated office with a fine old wooden desk lined in gold, a carpet of the finest threads under it, two large leather chairs, and a fireplace spitting in the corner, Dean Schatten sat. She had kept the office updated while still leaving the feel it had when she first took this seat, her throne. She refused to have the fireplace covered over, and it was always lit.

"A couple of students in front of Asbury are selling..." the secretary's voice went into a whisper, as if this was some sin, "drugs."

"Send my security guards there at once." The Dean didn't look up from what she was writing, annoyed that her concentration was broken. "You can also go to the cafeteria and bring me my lunch. Take the stairs. Why you keep putting on weight is beyond me. Being fat is a choice, a lazy one. No man is going to want you. The elevator up here is off limits to you from now on. Stairs and an hour after work on the treadmill. This is Prescott not some Community College. Understood?"

"Of course," the secretary was holding back tears. "As you wish Dean Schatten."

TJ waited around the corner until the security guards came running out. He had a small bottle in his pocket with a rag because if he had to chloroform the secretary he would. He was going to speak to the Dean no matter what.

As he turned the corner, the door opened again. He ducked back, and all he heard was the secretary crying to someone on the phone as she pushed opened the doors to the stairs and made her way down.

The witch, Dean Schatten, had been left alone in her office.

TJ turned the corner and as slowly and quietly as possible, he made his way to the door leading into the Dean's office. He got shivers just from opening the door and closing it softly behind him. Witches in general were known for excellent senses and hearing. If she had any inkling he was coming, he could be ripped to parts next.

Nothing but silence. A silence that was not welcoming.

Dani was in her bright pink Victoria Secret bra and panty underwear set. She had opted to do an hour of Yoga before her nap. She was just finishing the child pose, went into prayer seat, and prayed for a minute as the soft music played behind her.

For my gay brother, may he not be bullied in high school now that I'm not there. For my father, may he recover from my mother's suicide, cease his drinking, and be there through my brother's hard time. For everyone on campus who is dying, may their souls be welcomed to the doors of Heaven. Allow me to remain a humble servant. Guide me in the right direction, and I will continue to do right by the Lord. Amen.

"Namaste."

Dani got up, shook herself out, and walked over to her computer as a message popped up. Dressing like she did attracted the wrong kind of attraction on campus from everyone. It was just a style. If this was NYC and she was in her 20s, no one would say anything, but she was at Prescott, a college in a small town. She was supposed to be dressing in pink like sorority girls or in jeans and college sweatshirts like everyone else.

Dani knew she only lived once. Yes, she prayed, but she believed earth was her only realm. Tight dresses, doing her hair up, and wearing dark makeup was her look. Others might call her a slut and judge her on her fishnets and high heels, but she didn't care. She didn't care in high school. All she cared for in high school was her gay brother. She had the entire senior football team watching his back as well as the junior team and half of the sophomore team. Now that she wasn't there, though, she worried for him.

"Hey baby. Wanna see the Italian sausage in my pants? Bet you like fresh meat." Dani read the message from TimBoner829 out loud before hitting shutoff on her computer. "I'll pass."

As the computer screen went dark, she caught her reflection in the screen. Maybe a shower before her nap. Her makeup was running from the yoga. What she saw next... It had to be almost seven feet tall and was reaching a monstrous hand towards her hair...

TJ didn't bother to knock; he just opened the door.

"We knock here," the old woman shook in her throne. "This isn't a barn. We knock!"

"Dean Schatten?"

The old woman looked up with an ancient face, crooked nose, and beehive of dark hair on her head clasped with a single ruby pendant. The displeasure in her eyes was obvious, and she waved a hand. TJ put his arms up expecting to be thrown against the door or worse. Instead, she was waving a hand for him to close the door.

"I saw you at that Kappa party a few nights back. Close the door, and sit down. You are lucky you are handsome. It's been a long time since a handsome man has freely come to see me." The Dean shot her angry looking eyes at the door to be closed and motioned with a hand decorated in jewels for him to sit in one of the plush couches. "Sit in the right one. The left one is for bad students and annoying parents; it's worn. The right one I save for visitors like you."

"Like me?"

A smile, was it a smile, spread across her evil face. The Dean put her pen down and sat back in her chair folding her thin arms around each other. She was in a dark gold dress that looked like it was made of real gold. Her tiny hands and arms were covered in various jewels and rings probably filled with powers TJ couldn't imagine.

"I'm not going to call you handsome again, sonny. Only one compliment per day, and that's more than I give any of my children," the old woman cackled. "You don't go to this school. You don't live in this town. You aren't even from around here. I'm an old woman, but my senses are right where they should be."

Right, TJ thought, where a witch's should be.

Dani tried to scream as the oversized hand covered her mouth. It was gloved, but due to years of decay and death, through it she could feel the cold skin of dead fingers. It spread its fingers back until they cracked open. Maggots crawled out of the cut and popped into her mouth.

Dani looked up at its face.

The giant of a man was missing an eye, and part of its nose had rotted away. One ear was barely hanging on, moving as he moved. The other eye was an oval of white, and it had no eyelashes or eyebrows. Its lips were forming into a grin. It had no teeth, and the skin around the lips was dripping off. There was nothing in its mouth but an empty abyss. It held its hand over Dani's mouth as the maggots crawled down her throat. She could feel them flipping around in her stomach.

The creature took one of her yoga bands and wrapped it around her neck so fast she didn't even have a second to scream. He then dragged her across the room while she kicked and kicked, but he was too strong and too big. She was utterly helpless.

"You know I have never had a death on this campus." The Dean was strumming her dark nails together as she rested her arms on her desk. "Most of these kids are here to actually learn. Get degrees. Go on and do better things in life. I have watched a president come from this school, countless CEOs and high reigning chairs of companies, high performance athletes, and scientists. Now in two days… two deaths."

In the corner of the room, her fire crackled and the blaze of it lit up in her dark eyes. She had a sneer on her face. TJ had a long knife in his shoe. He figured slicing off her head or a perfect strike to the heart would do the trick.

After all, witches are human. Right?

"I'm Dean Lorena Schatten," the old woman held out a jeweled hand. "Formalities are always appropriate in my book. Your name please?"

TJ didn't move from his chair because he had no plans of shaking this witch's hand. He knew for a fact if a witch touched your skin it was an invitation into your mind and sometimes, depending on their power, your soul.

"TJ."

The Dean waited for a second and then brought her hand back to the other one, twisting a ring on her finger and strumming them together again. Was she casting a spell? Was she about to have him torn apart? Maybe he should strike now, so he began reaching towards the long knife in his boot.

"Not your real name." The woman raised a drawn on eyebrow. "Before you get yourself in anymore trouble, how about a real full name?"

"Thomas Johnson Featherstone." TJ lied about his middle name. If a witch knew your full name, the spells she could cast and the damage she could do was irreversible. "Happy?"

"Featherstone?" The old woman searched her mind. "Featherstone."

The Dean continued to strum her fingers together in an unsettling beat as the fire in the corner spit and crackled. Witches, truly powerful ones, didn't need to speak spells out loud to release curses. They could simply think them and send curses as far as their power could reach. TJ was once told that it was like a muscle; the more you flexed it, the more it grew. He bet Witch Dean Schatten had been flexing this muscle for quite some time.

He had the knife out of his boot. He'd swing around her desk and slice her throat.

"Marguerite?" the Dean finally said, her eyes opening in surprise and her hand touching the ruby clasp at her hair, "as in Marguerite Featherstone?"

"That would be my grandmother."

"Thomas Featherstone!" The Dean clapped her

hands together, and the same awful smile tried to curl her lips. "We've met sweet boy."

"We... we have?"

"Oh, dear." The Dean shook her head, and immediately TJ's mind was thrown for a loop. This wasn't a witch's trick. This wasn't how witches tricked people. She would have put a spell on him by now. She would have done something to him. "It was soon after your poor parents had that car accident, a terrible tragedy. Marguerite and I go way back. We used to go out for drinks in NYC back in our 20s. I was at her funeral. That was truly a sad day. Your grandmother was one special and one generous lady. This ruby clasp in my hair was a gift from her for my sixtieth birthday. Marguerite's Theater was built in her name after all the grants and funding she put into this school, plus her love of theater. The new gymnasium we are going to construct will be called Featherstone Gymnasium. She would have a limo bring her to my lake house in her later years. I learned a lot from her. What... what in heaven's name brings you here?"

The monster of a man, the creature, the it, grabbed tape off of Dani's desk, and opened his hand over her mouth. He let as many worms and grubs and maggots as he could into it and taped her mouth shut. Still holding her by the yoga band around her neck, he smiled that awful smile again. Dani realized it wasn't skin falling from its lips, but it was maggots, and they were coming out of its eye sockets -

maggots and worms and grubs. The creature looked like it was crying maggots.

She went to scream, and as her teeth closed, she smashed down on the maggots and worms in her mouth and went to vomit only to swallow that all down. It dangled her like this for a minute or two while bouncing her on the yoga strap just over the floor. It bounced her up and down playfully as the maggots crawled around her mouth and stomach.

For the next five minutes, as if she was a doll, he smashed her head and jaw together, so she crushed on each and every maggot, worm, and grub that had fallen into her mouth, filling her stomach.

Dani was a play toy, and this creature was not done playing.

The creature took her by her hair and swung her around once, so she hit every piece of furniture in the room. It made sure that at least one bone broke in the process.

Then it stopped and put her on her knees.

It held her in place on the ground and slowly twisted her head around. Slowly, millisecond by millisecond, each bone, every tendon, and all the skin cracked, broke, and snapped. The monster of a man, the creature, the it that bled maggots from its eyes, ripped her head right off her body.

Brad had been slaughtered by a machete in seconds. Joe was ripped apart in seconds. Dani's death took over twenty minutes - twenty minutes of maggots in her mouth, being toyed with and dangled, leading up to a grand finale with her head being slowly turned and ripped off of its socket.

It had meant for her to suffer.

When Dani's roommate came back into the room, all she could do was scream and scream and scream and scream. Across the walls written in Dani's blood was a math formula that only someone of Dani's mental caliber could solve.

TJ didn't know what to say. This was no witch. Dani had said it maybe an hour ago. Don't judge the book by its cover. He had. This was just an old, old woman who had been contorted and twisted into something that looked like a witch. In fact, she had known his grandmother and been good friends with her.

He even remembered the ruby clasp in her hair. His grandmother had once said she was sending it off as a gift to a good friend. Ugh, lie and lie quick, TJ.

"I heard about the campus murder. I knew how close you were to my grandmother. I guess I was a little embarrassed to come meet you after you caught me at the sorority party last night."

"Hush," the old woman waved her hand, and that evil smile, that wasn't evil at all, crossed her ancient lips. "Who can say no to girls like Clarissa and Melody? Forgive me for giving off such a terrible first impression. I was just doing my job. You know what they say? How they are as a husband is different than they are as a friend. Well, as I am as a disciplinarian is much different than what lies below this chest. I have a large family. I wish you were attending this school. My grandson Kevin, I helped him get in, but he has had trouble fitting in from childhood. I gave birth to five children. Four were stars who raised great kids who left this school to do great things. The fifth was a nasty woman. She never treated Kevin like a child should have been. Brad would have helped him. Talk about a rare bird. That boy would have helped him actually feel part of this school… this world. Now he's alone in that room. If you were here, would you be that kind? Or, is that just a rareness we find? Would you see Kevin and invite him to your lunch table, or would you make fun of him with everyone else to fit in?"

TJ thought about it, really thought about it. He probably would have judged Kevin, judged him harshly and hated him on site instead of getting to know him. Humans. We would be better off blind, Dani was right. TJ would have smelled him, saw the mess he had on his side of the room, and watched him stuff his face with pizzas. He would have wanted nothing to do with him.

"Don't answer that, deary." Dean Schatten looked over at the fire. "People call me the Witch Dean, but they don't know how much good I do or how charitable I am. It doesn't matter. I know who and what I am. Self-awareness is a gift a few of us have. Let the students fear me and my family love me. Maybe if I wore all pink all the time people would think I was good, right?"

"Right."

Wait.

TJ kicked opened Clarissa's door, even though 'do not disturb' was written in pink on her marker board.

In the middle of the room on the floor, Clarissa was surrounded by candles. In the middle was a crudely chalk drawn circle of symbols of the occult. Her eyes were rolled back into her head, and she was chanting in Latin.

She's in the middle of a curse, good. Witches can be killed mid-curse if they are weak. Clarissa was twenty something, so if she had been practicing, she had only been practicing for a short period of time. This had nothing to do with the Dean wanting her grandson to win student of the year, and this had nothing to do with Kevin at all.

Clarissa wanted to win student of the year and was slowly killing off her competition. TJ walked around her. It was as if she was in her own tornado. Her blonde hair was whipping around her, and the fire of the candles was spinning together to close the circle. Devil marks and demon symbols were roughly drawn on the floor. An eye was in the middle of the circle, a dead man's eye. A knife was in her hand. Now that she had no sleeves on, it was apparent that she had cut herself dozens of times. Dozens of offerings. What else had she done? What else had she been responsible for?

He got on his knees right in front of the fire circle and called out.

"Clarissa!"

Her eyes rolled back into place, and for a split second she attempted to put on her sorority girl smile, that beautiful smile, the grand smile that had almost fooled him into having sex with her and lose his virginity to a witch.

She quickly realized what he had just witnessed, and her eyes began to roll in her head again.

"Bad timing, TJ." Clarissa raised herself and snapped her fingers, which locked her door. "Bad. Bad. Bad. Bad."

Clarissa held up a hand, and TJ was forced up against the door.

"Why?" TJ had to ask. Clarissa had student of the year in the bag. He could even see her on the cover of the campus newspaper beaming with the award in hand.

"It's like..." Clarissa was on her feet, and the candles were back to just being lit candles. The hurricane of casting had ceased around her, but her voice was different, darker. The entire sorority girl thing had been an act. "A drug. Years ago a witch, Hecate, came to me. I would have thought she was nuts if she hadn't have met me in my dreams. She guided me and told me about how I'm a descendent of hers with some great power."

"Shakespeare? Like… Macbeth?" TJ's grandmother had him reading things like Ayn Rand and Shakespeare by nine. "Really?"

"It started with bringing my cat back from the dead." Clarissa was fixing her hair in the mirror and applying pink lip liner. "But… the power grows. I got perfect scores to get into this college with just a slice of my arm, sorority president with a cut on my wrist, and I was always attractive - but this? A deep cut into my leg bled enough for me to stand out."

"Blackest of magic requires sacrifices of blood, but you really aren't that smart are you? You made a deal with Hecate?"

Clarissa looked at him like he was dumb.

"Of course I made a deal with her. She gave me ultimate power!" Clarissa got back onto her knees and began to wipe away parts of the circle, drawing new ruins and new symbols. "I liked you. I would have taken your virginity with pleasure. Rare. Are you gay or something? Twenty something and a virgin, I would of drained a liter of your blood and then rode you. Oh the power that would have given me. The killer? This mental retard of a janitor died here a hundred years ago and stood almost seven feet tall. I found his grave, dug him up, and took his eye. It was enough for me to control him. You are about to meet him."

"Witches lie, Clarissa," TJ was still up against the wall. "Real ones do."

Clarissa crossed the room with a smug smile on her face.

"What? Because I'm the most beautiful girl you have ever seen and the most seductive creature you have ever encountered, I can't be a real witch? This is just the beginning Hecate said. Something is coming, something that will give me ultimate power and allow me to really release my power."

"You sorority girls really are awful, aren't you?" TJ easily pushed himself off the wall for her spell was weak. Hecate had lied to her. He took the knife from his boot and drove it into her heart. She looked up at him in surprise. "You aren't a real witch. You made a deal with some devil, and deals like that never follow through. You have no true power."

Clarissa looked at the knife that was in her heart, and TJ looked at her face one more time. Boy, had he learned a lot of lessons in the past few days. In her final breaths, her confidence was still beaming.

"I'll send you to hell."

"There is no hell," TJ pulled the knife out of her. "There is no heaven. You aren't going anywhere. You are going to spend eternity in nothing."

Burn the Witch. Burn the Witch.

Clarissa fell onto the witch's circle she had drawn. The candles all popping out one by one as her blood wiped over the crudely drawn chalk symbols.

Well, TJ thought, time to get out of here before I'm arrested.

TJ was back in his motel room on his bed with his face in his hands. Why was he doing this? Why was he traveling the country in search of the supernatural? So, his mirror as a child talked to him for six years telling him about the evil of the worlds, about a time before recorded history. So what? Maybe Dean Schatten was right. He was still in his early twenties, and he could go to college and make something out of himself. This wasn't his job. The mirror once told him the end of the world was coming. Why was this his job? So what?

"Bah. So what?" Across his motel room sitting on the wooden table with a leg lifted up and her chin resting on her hand was a witch. This one looked like a witch. She wore a dress and shawls of various colors all tattered and worn, probably cursed and blessed. Her hair was done up in dreadlocks and covered in gems and ties of many colors. Her skin was tan, but he couldn't tell her age. She could have been sixteen, or she could have been forty. Energy radiated off of her, this was the real deal. "Relax Thomas. I am the real deal. If I wanted you dead, you'd be dead."

"Who are you?"

"A friend." The witch was across the room in an instant sitting on the only chair in the motel room. "Spells be cursed this is uncomfortable. Didn't granny leave you enough money to stay in nicer places than this?"

"She left me enough money to buy that school I was just at… so, what? I killed a witch friend of yours, and now you are here to kill me?" TJ went for the knife in his boot. "Let's tango witch."

"Relax sparky. Take a lot more than a knife to kill me. My name is Gwen." The witch ran her eyes over him. "You. You had the pleasure of meeting my sister when you were a child."

"What do you mean?"

"Cassiopeia Dumont." Gwen waved her hand regally and sarcastically. "The most beautiful woman in all the ages. She was trapped by a voodoo priest in a mirror back in Greece when she was getting a little out of control. When you are that vain, being worshipped turns into an addiction. I hear her new claim to fame is 'Livin La Vida

194

Loca,' which was written about her. I keep telling her Ricky Martin likes men, but she won't let this one go."

"She tried to get me to free her for years. She wanted me to smash the mirror and bleed. My grandmother instilled in me as a kid that breaking a mirror is seven years of bad luck, and plus she wanted me to bleed on it. She gave up after a few years and then got bored and would just babble. Ramble on about a time before, about creatures of the night and the pits of the middle of the earth where awful creatures are born. Of how she was Aphrodite and…"

"… the angel of love?" Gwen rolled her eyes. "Vain and an over exaggerator. You are lucky you didn't free her, boy. A curse is placed on whomever frees her. I feel sorry for when that voodoo priest finds out that she's free. He's going to be after whomever freed her."

"Does he have a name?"

"Michael" Gwen rolled her eyes dramatically. "But I haven't seen him since Napoleon. Where The Lord of Voodoo is nowadays, I couldn't tell you."

"As much fun as this conversation is…" TJ had a lead on what sounded like a shape shifter in California. "What do you want?"

"To give you a present, a much better present than some shape shifter in California. It will be a few years, maybe more, maybe less. But… I'm done. This upcoming fight has no place for me in it. But, you… you will get a sign. You'll feel your bones tingle, or maybe a shooting star will hit you. You'll know when to travel to the Hotel Amira.

Then the battle is over, and the war has begun. Something wicked is coming this way."

In a spin of her cloaks, the witch was up against TJ. She smelled him, laughed to herself, put a hand on his head, and lowered him to the ground. Gwen placed both of her hands on either side of his face. She inhaled heavily and then exhaled. TJ's brain began to ache, and then it was a full on headache. It became so unbearable that he felt like his brain was exploding. The pain was paralyzing. It was too much to handle, and then he blacked out.

When he came to… Wow. He had been hung over once before. After one of his grandmother's parties when he was a kid, he had snuck a bottle of champagne to his room and drank almost half of it. The next day was awful, but this was worse. His head felt full of knowledge, of witches, of creatures, of demons, of Vega. It was full of things he would need days to try to understand and comprehend, weapons he needed, spells he needed to know, books he needed to find, the preparing he needed to do…

But one thing was clear.

One thing rang in his head louder than anything else.

He was here to kill them all when they came together.

He knew what he was.

A hunter.

Are You a Good Witch or Are You a Bad Witch?
NOW

It had been close to midnight, and Julia Baker was putting her head next to her husband's. He was a big man, standing over six feet tall, with a beard that she joked he cared more about than her. She swore that birds could live inside it. For their seventh year anniversary, she even bought him plaid and timberlands, which he got a huge kick out of. Aiden was that lumberjack she always wanted to curl up next to in bed.

Tonight was no different, Julia was snuggled up next to Aiden. Tomorrow, she needed to open the animal shelter up early. Aiden worked in marketing. No one seemed to have the ability to say no to that smile, so when they married, he insisted she do what she wanted. He told her to stay at home and pick a hobby or find any job; he just wanted her to do what would make her happy. So, Julia opened a no kill animal shelter, and it was the largest one in the state.

It was also how they wound up with ten cats. But, the house was large enough that they never seemed to get in the way. Aiden had built a large - almost child sized castle - outside for them and painted it in blues and greens. The cats seemed to like to spend their time there. Aiden had even built tiny beds for them with their names on the side. It was the details, the little things, which made her curl up tighter next to him each night.

Being a medium - witch - whatever aside, Julia's life had turned out as she had hoped. Growing up, she knew there was something 'off' about her. She aced every test, was able to dodge any bully, and knew who to make friends with and who to stay away from. The mistake she did make was telling her best friend that her mother was going to die walking across the parking lot after grocery shopping, and that night on the way out of the grocery store – well, you get it.

When she was about thirteen, her parents explained to her that she had a special aunt. She was an aunt who would always be around, no matter what, and that the two of them shared gifts - gifts that had skipped dozens if not more generations.

Shortly after Julia learned of her aunt, Gwendala of the Green, she came by for late night tea. Her parents stayed very quiet as her aunt told her everything she needed to know, which later became problematic because she should have told her everything...

Julia was falling in between that space of awake and asleep...

The whooshing sound came at her front door. The screen door rattled, and the porch boards creaked. Her husband went to jump up, but she put a hand on his chest. Gwen had told her to read his mind before marrying him, but Julia didn't need to because she could tell when someone was lying by just looking into their eyes. Another gift. He had never told her a lie. His eyes were so pure and kind they contradicted the size of him and his brute strength. Yes, he chopped wood for winter; yes, he went hunting; and yes, he would go on crazy adventures with his friends. Yes, his high roller job had sent him on countless business trips. But, she didn't need to know everything he was thinking, as long as his head was next to hers at the end of the day. Sometimes that's enough trust. If you need to read their minds to trust them, don't put that ring on your finger.

Julia would never invade Aiden's mind. Ever. Or go through his phone.

Julia got up and wrapped a robe around her body. She hadn't told Aiden about Gwen yet. That's a hard pill to swallow.

"One of the cats," Julia whispered into Aiden's ear. "I'll go give them some milk and spend a second on the porch because…"

"Fall is your favorite season, and you like it best when no one else is awake." Aiden smiled at her. "Go. Relax. When you come back… I might not let you relax."

He kissed her deep and held her for a second, that second where your eyes meet and connect, and you know you both are smiling. Julia sighed and walked out of the room. She made her way downstairs and opened the door.

"I think I could turn into a cat." Gwen was sitting on the porch, her leg up and her hand resting on her chin. She had on a new flowing jade gown, completely clear of the various gems and jewels that normally wrapped her threads. Gwen was untying a dread putting the strings and stones of various colors into a bag as she went. Julia looked at her hands, which had naturally aged over the years. Gwen still looked somewhere between sixteen and forty.

She was beautiful, a creature of another world, with no wrinkles. "Oddly in all of my years on these grounds, I've never felt the need to transform myself into anything. Take a shape of a bird and fly. A giraffe would just be fun. But, a cat wouldn't be my first choice. I'd turn into a unicorn with great pink wings and wander into some girl's birthday party. That'd blow everyone's mind. Fools."

God, Julia realized, *she looks years younger than me.*

"I will always look younger than you. Also, there is no God." Gwen didn't even look at her. She was gazing off in a specific direction. If one were to drive a few hundred miles, he or she would be at a certain hotel. "You hear what happened at that Ivy League School, Penisscout or something?"

"I felt... yes I saw it in my dreams. I just didn't feel the need to go. I have a lot of dreams about a lot of these things. But, I have a husband, and soon... hopefully a child." Gwen looked at Julia displeased with her answer. "What does this all mean?"

"That time is closing in. Another one of my old friends has popped up, trying to turn little girls into beginner witches. Part of the prophecy. An old witch shall rise with a coven before her feet as she lays laws. By the pricking of my thumbs, something wicked this way come..."

"What do you mean?" Julia felt like these were the things she should have been told. Everything was always on a need to know basis with her aunt, if that. "You are quoting Shakespeare..."

"Wasn't even her line but she claims it is. Bah, whatever," Gwen waved a hand and turned her eyes on Julia. Julia might as well call her niece or little cousin as aunt didn't suit her anymore. "Get over it. I'm young and supple, and you're in a bag that's slowly going to slouch and sag. Trust me. Living forever… not as cracked up as everyone seems to think it would be. I gave up on making friends back in the Egypt days. You get close to people, they die... repeat. Plus… you weren't around for the crusades. Now that was a mess."

"I dreamt of a boy… a Thomas. During 1997, I met him at his grandmother's, and he was just a little boy." Julia's house was on a hill overlooking the town and down into the city. Tonight the stars twinkled with the city lights - it was peaceful. Two days before Halloween, and it was the perfect weather. If it was daylight, a spray of oranges and reds would cover their eye site.

"In my dream, he was all grown up, as handsome as he was as a child. He skipped the college partying and has never had a drink or smoked a cigarette or tried a drug. Good looking and smart. A virgin at almost twenty-five. My dream was a tour through his mind, a ride I couldn't get off. It was the oddest thing… "

"He's a witch hunter," Gwen said as if this was a normal thing. "He's doing the same thing you are but without powers. I've met him. He has a role to play in this upcoming play. Looks like you might have found a connection with him, for in these upcoming times there has to be sides. If you were in his head, perhaps that in itself is a sign."

"A witch hunter? We are witches! Won't he hunt us?" Julia looked back to her house to where Aiden was probably naked in bed waiting for her. "I have a life, Gwen. I'm happy. I'm content… Is this something I have to worry about? I have a husband…"

"With eight inches waiting for you in his bed. No, I met the kid, and he's out to vanquish the demons that are beginning to walk around us. He can also tell the difference between what is good and what is evil, and what is good and what is right. I gave him enough knowledge to be very useful. You stay here." Gwen looked down. In all the years Julia knew her, she had never seen her look down. The top of her dreads were overlapping with gems and strings. "Julia… my days of doing this are done."

"Wait. What do you mean?" Julia went right up to Gwen and wrapped her wardrobe around her as a chill was rising off of her aunt. "Done?"

Gwen looked at Julia with the eyes of someone who had seen too much. Though her body was limber and her face was beautiful, something was off. The lengths of dreads were all wrapped together, almost overrun by the amount of gems and jewels and strands of various strings in them. There was no more room in her hair for another gem or another string. She was taking them out, letting her amber hair fall free from the dreadlocks that must have occupied her head for… Julia couldn't comprehend that math.

"You've called me aunt since you've known me, as your mother and her mother and her mother and her mother… going back to a time where I had a sister in my days. You, my dear, are from a bloodline that dates back before recorded history. A time where things were so much different. I was not even an adult when the skies opened. I stopped aging, as we all did, when our world came crashing down. Maybe it was in Vega's spell... or something else... bah whatever. Bunch of fools." Gwen looked back to Julia, "I'm tired, and there is something terrible coming. There is no coincidence that we have a hunter - maybe more than one - out there hunting down demons, the Enchantress running wild in Hollywood, a succubus heading this way, Hecate trying to replace her sisters, and more - much more - to either stop what's about to happen or help it begin."

"What do you mean?"

"Now." Gwen smiled, as if this was some game, but this was Julia's life, her job, her husband, and hopefully her baby; she wanted answers. "Where is the fun in that? You are no witch, a medium perhaps, but you have no true power. You weren't born like me and the others were. I wouldn't worry about a child, Julia. The ones with the gift are barren. Maybe adopt after all of this ends. Sorry. Right now, I'd worry about the world and stop worrying about yourself. This isn't just a blip on history's time-slot. This is a chaotic rumble that could end this planet. With that, I have to say goodbye. My time in this game is done, and I won't be there to see the final outcome. Forgive me for leaving you, but I'm leaving you with so much."

"Why! What are you doing?!" Julia got up and went to hug her aunt, but her aunt's arm shot up, her eyes turning a bright white. Her hands fell on Julia's hands, gripping them tight. "What's... what's going on?"

"Etsnen nan ran deunt talishia arunt tabllleite etsnen nan ran deunt talishia arunt tabbelitte…" Julia couldn't hear, she couldn't see, she couldn't move, and everything went black for a second. Gwen's hands were wrapped tight in hers as she began to mumble faster. The winds picked up around the two of them, whispers and screams circling wildly about them.

Stop.

There was a moment of utter peace, a single moment of just nothingness, of quiet, of no worries. Spring fields and meadows. Making love on the porch of a lake house. Laying a head on a shoulder watching a sunset during a hike. Being carried over the threshold of a new home and doing it right there on the floor. Then, a boom erupted from inside her body, and when she opened her eyes, her Aunt Gwen was gone.

Everything hurt. Everything was seizing up inside.

Julia stumbled against the porch, fell down, went to get back up, and collapsed. Her body began to seize and shake as if a deathly illness had overtaken her. Her entire body was shivering from top to bottom. A virus had taken over her body. It was so intense that her body shut down.

Darkness. Nothingness.

The next thing she knew, Aiden was carrying her up the stairs with a look of pure worry in his eyes. For such a big burly man, one who had punched a guy for grabbing Julia's behind at a bar, he cared so much, and it showed in those eyes. She relaxed, and when he saw her eyes were open, he smiled.

"Gave me a scare, little panda," Aiden said as he laid her back in bed, "Did you fall asleep out there? You were shaking. Are you ok?"

"No," Julia smiled and waited for him to come back into bed. Something was off. Something had changed. "I just got dizzy when I was outside. I don't know what happened, but let's hope it doesn't happen again. I'll see a doctor if it does. I'm just… overwhelmed with work and stuff."

Or my aunt basically tearing my body to shreds.

"Well," Aiden smiled that smile and went in for a kiss, "that's why I'm here."

Julia laughed as he tore her robe off, and they began to tumble in the sheets. She got on top of him and let her red hair down. She went in for a kiss, and they embraced and began the dance that lovers do. The windows were open with a chill coming in. As he bit her neck, she sighed and completely relaxed into him. Without realizing it, she flicked her hand at the window.

It closed and locked itself.

The Hotel Amira was the most famed hotel in all of California, the highest rated in the United States of America, and up there as top in the world.

A five star rating wouldn't cut it as critics couldn't praise it enough.

Patricia Allen wrote: "Stayed here with my family to get a much needed vacation in 1997. Staff could not have been friendlier, and the accommodations were endless. Had enough for the kids to do during the day, so we adults could enjoy the acclaimed spa. I have never seen a shower with 18 different nozzles and color changing lights with water falling over me. I was in heaven."

Amanda S. wrote: After a divorce, I came out here to take a breather and spoil myself, so I got a suite. Spent his money, the bastard. Three full rooms, a living room, a dining room, and a full master with a king bed. Elegant art and magnificent statues stretched the halls and the carpets - even in the hallways - must have cost a fortune. Ladies, swipe those credit cards at the gift shop. Who has Swarovski and Gucci shoes next to each other? Eat that you cheater!

Yes, it was well known that the Amira hotel was the decadent of decadence in California, and only the finest of staff was hired. Each was trained in every job for months and had to pass multiple tests. Staff had psychology evaluations, extensive background checks into their and their families' lives, blood tests, drug tests, and even hair follicle testing.

The pay itself was insane and the bonuses and incentives just kept on rolling in.

Sera normally worked the front desk, which she excelled at. She was mentioned on Yelp many times as being a highlight of a person's stay at the Amira.

"Warm, friendly, and just a perfect lady" - Ann Marie, 86, hello am I doing this right Houston Texas, wrote.

"Beautiful, smart, pretty, wonderful with kids, attractive." - Bob, 56, married, wrote.

"Was our wedding coordinator. As the bride, I literally was able to relax in the Amira's famous spa while Sera handled everything. I had not even met the girl before, and everything was not just perfect, it was flawless. Brides, if you want a true Xanax to handle your wedding details, Sera is a godsend." - Alysa, 28, Las Vegas, wrote.

Tonight Sera was in a suite entertaining a group of kids as their parents were all at their business gala, which would be ending in 20 minutes. The hotel was over booked this weekend for the business meeting and for the next as an archeologist was coming to unveil a discovery he made in the depths of Egypt. A grand ball was to be thrown, and Sera didn't know what job she'd have for that night.

Being children of rich parents normally equated to Sera getting brats, but luckily these kids were calm. They sat and played on their iPads and with each other while Sera played along with them. She always let the kids win, but Sera knew she should win a few times and teach them life lessons. However, she didn't have the heart to destroy a four year old girl in Penguin Cuddle Fest.

"Read us a story," a young boy named Jared said. "There's a whole bookshelf over there."

So there was. Sera hadn't noticed it before. She enjoyed reading books to children. You could make up voices and really get into booing the villains and cheering on the good guys.

"Pick any one you want."

All the kids looked at each other.

"Just pick the one with the prettiest binding."

All the kids nodded and ran over to the bookshelf. Sera gazed out a floor length window in the suite. New rugs had just been put in that exposed an expensive wood shined floor, and the Hotel Amira had no fog around it tonight. You could see directly all the way over to the ocean, and tonight a beautiful sunset had made the room sparkle.

All of the expensive vases and candle sticks had been hit by red and purple lights that winked and shined.

The energy here had been good.

The littlest girl was wearing a fairy princess outfit - ah to be four - and was struggling to carry a big black book with a gold binding over to Sera.

"I got that," Sera laughed and took the book from the little girl. She picked her up and sat her on her lap, "Want to help me read."

"I can't read yet," the little girl whispered in her ear. "Can you read it for us?"

"Yes! Read it for us!"

All of the children sat around Sera in a semi-circle. The book was huge, the binding was gold and jagged, the cover was pitch black, and the gold title was just an symbol she had never seen. Sera touched the book, and she swore she felt it gasp for breath.

At that moment, Janet McAllister stormed into the room.

"Tonight was a travesty! Travesty! I might as well have thrown the moon into the earth and called it a win!" She was in a blue ball gown. The other parents began to come into the room and exchange goodbyes while retrieving their children, but Janet was already removing the clippings from her hair. "They should have had you out there, Sera. Lauren Mortina cannot work a function, and this is our eighth year doing it here. The food was delayed, the soup was cold, and the cake was not edible. Come here, Jenny."

Janet lifted the little 'princess' off Sera's lap.

"Next year you will plan it for us like usual. The past three years were perfect; the other girls before you were just as incompetent. Whose bright idea was it to have you watch children!? You should have been doing what you do best! If something is broke, don't fix it." She opened her purse and counted out a thousand dollars. "There is also no way you made the money you should have working our party and babysitting these little munchkins."

"Oh, Mrs. McAllister!" Sera had never seen someone count out that much money so casually before. "I can't accept that."

"Sera," Janet counted out five hundred more and put in into Sera's hand. "I hate people. I just do. There are annoying horrible selfish… but I like you. As always, the owner, your boss was a grump. I'll tell him how awful Lauren was, how fantastic you are, and how he must give you a raise. You are a special girl, Sera. But that's enough compliments for the year for me. I bid you goodnight dear. Keep that energy."

Sera nodded, took the $1500 and the large book, and left the suite.

As she walked down the hallway, she took in the new look. They had just modernized it with a whole mirror vibe, well this floor anyway. Each floor had a different vibe to it with mirror furniture, walls, lamps, silver statues, odd knick knacks, and a rug of black and white swirl.

Sera found a couch and sat down. She tried to fit the money into her wallet and threw the overstuffed wallet into her backpack. She looked up at her reflection. For an almost nineteen year old girl, she worked a hardcore job. Her mom was an alcoholic and not in the picture, and her dad had left. Sera had been on her own since the age of fifteen. She had landed this incredible job, a studio apartment, and was planning from there.

"Being beautiful doesn't hurt either," Janet had told her one year. "Young and beautiful are two deadly combinations."

A compliment from Janet was like a compliment from Gordon Ramsey - take it directly to the bank.

"Ouch!"

Sera had cut herself on the edge of the book, and a drop of blood hit the book. She wiped it up quickly. She never took breaks, so she decided now was a good time to take a fifteen minute breather. Her 'grumpy' employer would let her take an hour if she wanted or even a day, for she never took days off.

Sera went to an employee exit staircase, sat down, and opened the book.

Pangea

I know we know, what we know. Told in tales of times both now and long ago. Written down on pages upon pages to wind following our youths through the ages. Let me tell you of a time, which has been erased from both you and me.

A grand kingdom that spread the land, covering it from end to end. Water filled the rest of this spinning globe, only one giant land. They were one. They were whole.

A people who all could open up their hands and do great things that no one knew, you now can. Some could move things with their mind, others could make gardens grow before your eyes, and others decided to send fire flying through the skies.

Each member of these lands had their own special powers in their hands. There were a few, though, who could do more than any others were capable of doing - a few who seemed to master land, sky, water, and sand.

All seemed well until others were born... hungry for the blood of others around.

A balance seemed to be needed for those who craved love and for those who wanted to kill and spread disease. But then out of the darkest of the darkest nights in a fire that people had spent days upon days to put out, a sound exploded across the sky.

A terror of terrors possible began to rise.

Vega.

Her power sucked the powers of all those around, making her the most powerful witch in the kingdom. They even gave her a twisted dark crown.

Sera, a maid is coming, so we shall continue more later. Stay white. Stay bright. Stay away from the beasts of the night.

"Sera?" One of the maids was coming up the stairs with a fresh set of towels, only the fluffiest towels at the Amira. "You ok?"

"Yes," Sera closed the book shut, and it sighed. "I just think I need to call it a night. Another long day at the Amira."

"You telling me."

The maid made her way up the stairs. Sera opened the book, but it was empty. All of the pages were empty. As she closed the book and held it tightly against her chest, she felt her heartbeat against it, and the book was beating back with her. Warmly.

Hecate stood at the door to a coffee house.

Well, that isn't exactly accurate. Hecate had inhabited a body of a sixteen year old, emptied her out, strung her like a puppet, and was currently spinning the strings inside of her. Deep within where this girl's heart used to be, Hecate sat spinning a spinning wheel, making this vessel move.

Hecate was staring at Julia Baker with an extreme amount of envy. There sat an actual blood relative of Gwen of the Green, one of the most powerful witches of all time - well, more of a sorceress if we were being exact. Hecate looked at her young, borrowed hands and sighed. Julia had to be in her thirties, but the beauty was natural and real. Hecate, in her true form, was nothing more than an ancient hag. Her own fault.

Before this apocalypse, she had one job to do: build an army of witches to meet Vega at her rising point. So far, three had killed themselves trying to use magic, and her

212

most promising pupil yet, Clarissa… Hecate couldn't mentally connect with her anymore.

But Julia… If she could get Julia to meet his Great Lord the Voodoo King, she might see reason, and if she had an inch of her aunt's power in her, maybe together they could recruit young witches, build the coven twice as fast, and fulfill the prophecy.

As Hecate went through the door, she felt the air between her and Julia, something… power… she smelled of power that she couldn't possibly possess. This might be the witch she needs. As she took a step, the power radiating off Julia was so enlightening that she almost needed sunglasses.

It was so white.

Hecate cracked her neck, stretched her hands, and began to spin the wheel. A wind gusted throughout the coffee house, and before Julia could even notice Hecate, she was gone.

Julia looked over at the door, shuddered, and zoned back out. She sipped on her hot chocolate and sighed. A minute ago she was debating kitchen curtain colors and birthday gifts for Aiden. They had also finally discussed the fact that it was time… for a child.

Julia had been sitting in that spot for hours debating how to go about telling Aiden that she was barren and fill him in on the details of her aunt. It would be easier now that she could…

She twisted a hand about, and outside a gigantic pile of leaves began to twirl together and dance about each other. Not one color touched the next as they twirled higher and higher into a tornado of fall. Everyone in the coffee house was watching it as the wind does weird things. Julia, though, focused her mind on the tornado of leaves and turned it into a blast of flames.

Ashes fell to the earth. Everyone in the coffee house was trying to catch this on their cell phones, while she sighed again and put her head in her hand.

I'm a witch, she thought as one would admit they were gay to themselves or that they have a drug problem, *a full blown witch. Thanks Aunt Gwen.*

Gwen had her hand around Hecate's neck, and they were on top of a mountain. It was freezing and Hecate was shaking drastically. Gwen just smiled as her nails wrapped around the girl's neck. Understanding was in her eyes.

"You'll leave her alone," Gwen squeezed her hand as Hecate kicked. "You dumb fool."

Gwen released Hecate and flung her to a pile of rocks. The sky was void of clouds, and you could see valleys upon valleys - they were literally in the middle of nowhere, somewhere without cellphone reception, Wi-Fi, or any interference.

Gwen and Hecate were both at their most powerful. Hecate began to swirl her hands, and fire began to form. Gwen shot a look over her way, and from the underground, a rupture of thick vines with thorns attached themselves to Hecate's hands and legs.

"Ouch!"

"You are much younger than me. Fire balls? I will build a forest on top of you before you can even collect enough flames to muster." Gwen wasn't even looking at Hecate, but the vines were tightening and growing in vast number. In minutes, she would be buried below the greenery. Hecate closed her hand as the fire dissipated, and the vines crawled back into the ground.

"A war is coming you dumb witch." Hecate was bleeding and waved a hand over the wounds on her arm and legs as they vanished. Getting back to her heels, she faced Gwen. "Ugh, this vessel is human you idiot. Blast me open, and you can face a hag, but I don't want to fight you. I know you'd win Gwen - you are much more than a witch - we are past these squabbles. The battles are done, and real wars are coming. Creatures that I thought were dead are coming back, and they all seem to want Vega to rise. They hate this world, these humans, and this terrible civilization they created. We can't take Vega. No one can."

"Where have you been these past four hundred years?" Gwen slowly circled Hecate, looking her up and down. "You look like a prostitute. You've been alive and kicking before humanity, and this is your choice of outfit? I figured a hag like you would pick a more… mature vessel. You are a witch, not a succubus. You don't need to lure…"

"Listen I like to look good. So, thanks, and you look like you smell of patchouli and smoke weed." Hecate snapped back. "The signs are all here. Cassiopeia, her grand enchantress, has been living it up in Hollywood. The Succubus Queen is making her way to California. I've been dreaming of the Hotel Amira. Of hunters. Of white and black witches. But I have seen more evil in my dreams than good. More horrors than pleasantries. By the time Vega rises, we shall all fall if we don't stand with her."

"You didn't answer my question."

"I've been visiting various friends of ours. His Lord Master Voodoo King wishes an audience with you…"

"Lord Master and King now?" Gwen smiled and let down one of her dreadlocks to pluck a gem out of it into her bag. Half of her hair was free of the strings and gems along with the dreads. Beautiful amber hair was beginning to occupy the majority of her head. It fell down her back and was truly a magnificent color. "You can tell his greatness that we will meet at the world's end. Leave my niece alone. Your nose smelled something back there?"

"Yes," Hecate snapped her eyes angry, "her power. She has more power in her than I do. How could she grasp that much…"

Gwen stepped back and took a bow.

"Oh, you stupid bitch." Hecate kicked a rock with anger but just stubbed her toe. Gwen laughed. "You gave her your powers?! She knows nothing of the storms coming and nothing of the thunders that will rupture these grounds. Nothing about the fate that is destined upon us all!"

"What exactly is inside that vessel of yours?" Gwen was close and smelling at the witch's neck. "I bet it is old school magic. You being the hag you are, spinning this girl inside through your strings at a spinning wheel. If I were to rip her open, I would find you. I would find you spinning away, an ancient hag."

"Get away from me!" Hecate stepped back unevenly. "Julia knows nothing of the world from which we came. How can she help? You might be one of the oldest and most powerful of all the beldams, but Vega will crush you. She will destroy your white witches, your Julia, your hunter."

"Exactly, you stupid bitch. Foolish child." Gwen raised a hand, and the ground began to slowly rumble. Gwen smiled to herself as Hecate couldn't balance properly in her vessel. Hags. Old ancient magic. Low on the chart of power. "You have in your tiny brain that Vega will rise, and the earth shall fall with you and others by her side? History repeating itself all over again - this isn't destiny or fate. We are writing this story as we go. I've been around just as long as you, and I know... I know not everything is going as planned. It is written that an ancient witch will have a coven at the door's end. Where are your baby witches? I heard about the one at the university. A hunter ended her before she could even perform an entrance into your coven. You stand alone, Hecate. We've been talking about prophecies and destiny. Vega is coming - that much I know. The rest you don't even know. You can't. Nor will I be there to help you. For a hag, you are one worthless, spoiled child. There isn't a haze yet or even a drizzle. The skies are still clear, for it hasn't even begun to happen yet."

"Then help me!" Hecate pleaded as Gwen vanished. "Curses!"

Hecate stood at the top of the mountain and looked down over the land. Where in the stars did she bring her? She was overlooking valleys and fields and mountains and hills. All of it was untouched by man, free from technology and industry. A rare site to see, Hecate remembered when the world wasn't so crowded, when land was everywhere and people were minimal. She also remembered the dinosaurs, which was an interesting time.

It was beautiful. Hecate smiled for a second, and then her brain began to ache. Her master was calling her. Obedience. Orders. Consistency. Now.

"Argh." Hecate felt his power about her. She couldn't teleport, but he could, and in a flash of blue screaming flames, she was gone.

"I will do as you request, master." Hecate was on her knees in front of a chair, dark robes rolling down stone steps. Hecate went to raise her head, but with a flick of his dark hand, her head was lowered.

"You do not look upon me," the Lord Voodoo King boomed arrogantly. "Bacteria sprawled at my feet. The prophecy speaks. You should have a coven by now. Where are your witches? Where is the coven that will circle me when Vega rises?"

"Master, the book is lost. These were things yelled and screamed while Vega raised her arms and had us at our feet. What… what if we are wrong? What if she is returning to just destroy this world and not fix it? What if she plans to destroy us all, for putting her in that box…?"

"Enough." A hand boomed on the arm rest of his skull throne, and from a corner, bones rolled down to

Hecate's feet. Hecate wasn't allowed to meet his eyes, and she wasn't allowed to speak until spoken to. His power was so great, she literally could not lift her head. He had given her this young girl's vessel, allowed her to wrap her hag strings up in her, and in there she spun. "Go. Get Gwen of the Green's niece. Do what it takes to make that woman a witch worthy of this fight. Mia the Succubus Queen is opposing us, Gwen is opposing us, and Cassiopeia will pick whatever side looks like it'll win. Gwen will release him, Hecate. She will release him, and when he spreads those dark wings…"

"More witches, master."

"Get away from my sight," the man growled dangerously. "Be useful Hecate. Be worthy of living, and I will keep you alive. If you fail me, I will snap one of those strings you are weaving, and you'll just be a hag needing a lot more than a vessel to cast any magic worth fighting against. Be gone."

He flicked his hand, and in a flame of blue, she was gone.

"Aiden?" Julia called upstairs for the third time. "Your truck was in the driveway. I know you are home."

Through her ears, a sound meant only for her, a wicked witch cackled.

Julia grabbed the side of her kitchen center table, stumbled on it, and caught herself before falling. Two of her cats were meowing angrily at her, and the rest of her cats were jumping up and down and around the kitchen all hissing at once.

"Oh no."

Julia felt like she was heading through quicksand. As she reached the stairs heading to the second floor, her feet moved through the ground as slowly as possible. She started to climb the stairs, and it seemed as if they would never end. A tiny black cat jumped on her shoulder. It was like walking through honey. There were only a dozen steps. But now? One hundred. Julia began to cry as she neared the top, the tiny kitten licking the tears from her face. As she finally hit the top of the stairs, she turned towards her bedroom.

A young girl, a teenager, with short cut hair and hooker boots was in her bedroom.

Hecate was standing in front of her bed where Aiden was sound asleep, a small smile on her face, his arms wrapped into a pillow like it was Julia. Hecate began to mumble in a language Julia now knew - a devil's tongue - the whispers of the center of the world where fire spins, flames explode, and the darkest of creatures rise.

Hecate raised a hand and in it began to spin a dark orb, filled with screams and fire that only Julia seemed to hear as Aiden was moving. Julia tried to move faster towards the room, but her legs were being dragged. Hands began to reach out of the walls grabbing at her red hair, pulling her back, and holding her back from Aiden.

Julia tried to scream, but a hand slammed over her head, and the cackle rang throughout her head again. A true witch's cackle. The cackle you hear on recordings of Halloween and in *The Wizard of Oz*. A cackle of pleasure.

The orb in Hecate's hand expanded, and it exploded forward. Hands began to pull Julia apart and drain the power from her directly into Hecate.

The kitten bit her ear.

"Fuck! Fuck! Fuck!" Julia screamed as she woke drenched in sweat. Aiden terrified, twitched and fell off the bed, a gigantic thump. He was a giant in many ways. "Oh my God! Aiden!"

He got up, a look of utter confusion in his eyes.

Julia threw her arms around him and shook her head. If she were to touch her ear, there would be a tiny drop of blood from where the kitten bit her.

"Make love to me." Aiden looked confused at this, as he tended to perform this normally. "Make love to me like you are never going to see me again."

He asked no questions. His eyes grew hungry, and he tossed her into the bed. As they made love, she exuded as much sensation as she could from herself onto him, a protection spell, binding him to her. No matter what, no matter where, she would know if he was in trouble. She would come running.

Inside a room that was decorated in fine gold furniture and grand red drapes with matching carpets, a fireplace roared from behind a golden encasement. The entire room was lined in gold.

Lord Voodoo King stood over a pot of virgin blood, a cauldron that rose from the ground with a circle of tortured souls surrounding it. Cloaked and circling it, he looked into it and growled angrily. He needed every fighter he could on his side. He needed every warrior he could. His powers were great. He was one of the original born, one of the original that first opened their eyes onto the valleys of the earth.

Across from him stood an equal, Abaddon his brother. Both had beautiful sets of wings, the type religious fanatics would call the arch angels when they accidentally made appearances throughout the ages. They both shared so many things that it made sense for them to join forces and build a kingdom as more and more creatures of power began to form. But no friendship lasts forever, and when The Voodoo King discovered his true powers… the two had a battle that broke their bond forever.

Would he be at the Hotel Amira? He did not know. He and Abaddon haven't exactly been in touch throughout the years. Hecate was a regular visitor and an annoying one. She was so ugly in her real form that he insisted she take these virgin's bodies.

Cassiopeia would be an issue. Once he found the one who had let her go, there would be a great punishment. Too much power for one so vain, never put to good use, never used properly. That was one powerful spell, and many players went into tricking her to get into that mirror. The world had been better. He had seen her dancing her life away in Las Vegas and in Hollywood since she broke free. She lived in a huge mansion with a harem of men for herself. A witch with no purpose was beyond selfish, but she was not a witch but a powerful sorceress - even worse.

Mia the Succubus would be another problem. Even in her tiny form her powers were incredible. Once she grew to over ten feet of madness with those wings and those teeth... The Voodoo King let on a shudder. He didn't know how to fight let alone kill a succubus.

Vega would be a wild card. The woman couldn't have been more beautiful in her original form with long tumbles of raven hair, dark wild eyes, ivory skin, and a body that even the Enchantress envied. But she was hungry, and in a world of power, she quickly began to figure out a way to transfer others powers to herself. Don't misunderstand - her victims kept their powers, but now she had their powers as well. It was a form of witchcraft that no one had seen before... and at a certain point... when you fill yourself with too much power...

"Your majesty." The changling had returned in the form of some Abercrombie and Fitch model with a large bag filled with a virgin on his back. "May I bleed her now, or do you wish to save her?"

"Bleed her above." The Voodoo king motioned above his bird bath of blood where a young girl was hanging. She was completely pale. "That one is empty. I need... I must summon back-up plans. Hecate isn't building a coven, no one is gathering, and there has been no great catastrophe showing current leaders are unworthy. It's been millenniums. Witches have always given the same prophecies, but now that we have arrived, none of them are coming true. Cut out the organs from the last girl because they can be used, and then burn her body in the furnace. Place the other girl up and bleed her."

The changling, with his Abercrombie shirt and plastic looking tan, removed the young girl who was strapped in with multiple leather straps - a contraption meant to be a sex swing that the Voodoo King had fashioned into his own blood dispenser. The new girl was placed above, he waved a hand, and the changling prepared her. When he was done, he shoved a tube with a spout in her neck and turned as his cauldron needed more blood. As her blood began to drip, the Voodoo King shot a look at his changling.

"Be gone."

"As you wish master." The Abercrombie model stepped back into darkness and was gone. The Voodoo King met the changling back in 1800s England. He didn't know if it was a man or woman, but it shed its skin at will. A very useful talent. It helped that the changling was deranged and worshipped evil, falling knee to the Voodoo King and his plans was swift and easy.

The Voodoo King took a knife and cut it against his own hand. The cloak over his head almost touched the blood bath as he bent low and licked his tongue into it. He raised a hand with a dark metal ring of a serpent over the bath.

"Der Mensch ist Gott." The octaves of his voice began to separate as he began to invoke. He waited a moment. A moment longer. "Der Mensch ist Gott!!"

The words circled about themselves and dove into the cauldron as it began to bubble. The small people on the outside, the faces of agony, and the outstretched tiny arms all began to bleed. Deep within the bath of the virgins' blood, the answers came in tones and grunts of pleasantness.

"Der Mensch ist Gott."

The Voodoo King felt the words pass into him, over him. They were battle wounds and attacks. He had an army inside and was prepared to hold them at bay. These were the forces of the depths. Those which lurk in the core of everything we walk upon. They were calls from the fire pits of the burning sphere of the center of our Earth.

"Wir sind Menschen!" The Voodoo King called down upon the bubbling of blood as he turned the spout in the girl's neck allowing her to flow freely. Slowly as this engagement of conversation between what we see and know and what lies in the darkest of the dark, the virgin blood drained from the raised up cauldron.

"Sein ist das Haus des Schmerzes! Sein ist die Hand die verletzt!" A retort, an angry one, a call back that wasn't a welcome one. But the Voodoo King expected that because after all, he was dealing with the beasts of the deep.

"Wir sind Menschen!" he called into the now spinning pit of blood. He cut his hand again and allowed his blood to flow down into the spin. A yawn escaped from the cauldron.

"Gott ist der Mensch."

"Wir sind Gotter!!!" There was one final call, and everything stopped. He turned off the spout of the neck of the girl. He never looked them in the face. He knew duct tape was over her mouth and eyes. The changling would wrap them up, so he could just pretend like they were pigs he was bleeding. She was nothing more than a blood bag to conjure the forces he needed. He had no need to know her or what he has taken as his offerings to the deep.

The blood drained completely from the cauldron, and all that was left was a ring. A newly forged ring, onyx and glittering with a giant red crystal in the center. As he lifted the ring, he held it to the light, and inside he saw them bouncing around in darkness.

Good, he thought. *I have my army if necessary. I do not need a witch's coven or any of those other prophecies. If Vega doesn't want a partner, I will take her on myself with my army of demons!!*

"Michael?" A soft female voice came from a top of a stairs to the basement where he stood. "Hunny?"

Quickly, he closed his eyes and waved his hand around the room whispering in a calming tone that lifted the negative energy from the room and glamoured it.

"Everything is not as it seems, and when she looks at me, all she sees is dreams."

What was a second ago a Voodoo King's practicing lair complete with a raised blood cauldron and a virgin bleeding above it, a throne, skulls and bones, a shelf of herbs and jars filled with everything from eye balls to fetuses, now was a *suburban* basement with a pool table and a huge work station with all the tools that Home Improvement would have had.

Down the steps, in a nice fall dress with her hair recently done, a lovely woman made her way into the basement. Michael, a devilishly handsome man in his mid-thirties with blonde hair that curled with one small curl that always fell right on his forehead, turned from the work bench. The bluest of eyes beamed and glistened, and he spread a smile a dentist would envy, complete with two dimples on each side. He was shirtless. He could walk around shirtless, and no ladies would ever complain. His arms were those of a man who cut his own wood and built his own furniture.

"I've been calling you from upstairs. The Hendersons will be here in half an hour, and you still need to shower darling." She kissed him on his lips and sat on his lap. "I'd say stop playing around down here, but the more you build things, the bigger your arms get."

"I'll jump in the shower now, Sarah." Michael turned back towards his pool table with Hecate on his mind. The witch was weak but could possibly play a bigger role in all of this than he anticipated.

"Hey hun. In the next few weeks, I have to do some business at the Hotel Amira in California. I'd say let's bring the kids…"

He knew her answer before he mentioned it.

"You can't keep taking them out of school!" Sarah laughed. "They missed a month three years ago with our impromptu month visit to Egypt. Go, keep that tan. I won't complain."

Michael sighed as his wife made her way up the stairs. Over the millenniums… that he had been on this earth, he had fallen in love three times. Once during the times of Jesus, once during early 1800s England, and then again six years ago. It brought him so much pain to watch his wives grow old, glamouring them so they believed he was growing old too, and then burying them. He had a romantic side, and Sarah and he were only six years into this dance. He didn't know how it was for the others, but he felt each second, each minute, each moment. Did years feel like a blink of time to them? Did a thousand years feel like a week?

Nevertheless.

He needed to meet Vega on the field, for Sarah and his two children couldn't die, not like this. He'd fight for his family.

A tear formed at his eye at the thought of it, as a fifteen year old girl lay in straps of leather above a blood cauldron. A single drop of blood fell from the spout and into the bowl below.

Sera pulled her car into her apartment complex and sighed as she dropped her swipe key outside the car.

"Shit." She went to open the car door and hit her head. "Ouch."

She picked up the swipe card just as she closed the door on her foot. She yelped in pain as she got a slight electric shock as she swiped the card. The gate started to open and then just fell shut on her car.

What in heavens is going on?

Her car began to smoke from the outside, so she jumped out of it grabbing her bag and the book before she did. As she backed away, the car exploded, sending chunks of it flying everywhere. The explosion flipped the car over onto the first parking spot on top of what happened to be a cranky man's new Porsche.

People began to run out of the building. A couple that lived above them, the single guys from down the hall, a blonde she had never seen before, the old woman who lived in the first apartment. Most just watched from their windows.

Running towards her was Ryan, her boyfriend. He was shirtless, so she slowed that moment down in her head... It was like watching *Baywatch* as he was a typical California surfer dude. "Sera... is that your car?!" Ryan pushed a strand of long brown hair away from his face. He had been her boyfriend for two years, and she had recently - reluctantly - let him move in with her. "What happened?"

"I..." Sera looked at him, and something in her mind opened. "Yes... what took you so long to get out here?"

"Call of Duty..." Ryan dropped his head. "Also, I hid all the bongs and weed in case the cops came in. I don't want my Heller Kush to get taken. That stuff is hard to get."

He put one tan and toned arm around her, a coy fish sleeve tattoo wrapped to his chest and on the other side a bunch of stars aligned in his astrology symbol. Ryan pulled Sera in tight, but she didn't feel comfort as she had just watched her car explode.

"Who was the blonde who ran out of the building?"
"Blonde?"

"Right after my car exploded." Sera looked up into Ryan's big brown eyes; another strand of long hair had fallen in front of his face. "Some blonde girl I never saw before ran out of the building."

Ryan just shrugged, but Sera didn't like the energy on this. Did the blonde have something to do with her car? With everything that just had happened? Was this some sort of terrorist attack? Emergency vehicles were sending their sirens in the sky, and soon the apartment building was surrounded by police, ambulances, and fire trucks.

A police officer was talking to Ryan, who Sera was sure was stumbling over his statement. He never was a good liar. Another police officer approached Sera.

"Miss, that's your car right?" The officer looked tough and angry, as if he had left off shift and had to come back on for this call. "Wanna tell me what happened?"

"No." Sera looked up from the ground at him. "Write up a fancy report, and leave me alone."

She put her hand to her mouth. Did she really just speak that way to a police officer?

He smiled, nodded his head, and walked away. From her backpack she felt a thumping, like a heartbeat.

Sera pulled the black jagged edged book out and opened it.

Chapter 1
Your powers have begun.
End of Chapter 1.

Sera flipped through the pages, and there was nothing else in the book. She sat down on the lawn while the rest of the people in the apartment building filed out to get a look at her car. Mechanics would claim they had never seen anything like this before as there was nothing wrong with the car. It was as if something inside of it, like a bomb being set off, just let loose.

When you are in the learning process of anything, you'll screw up a few times here and there.

This was Sera's first... and only... screw up.

Cassiopeia Dumont was at some VIP room in some club in Las Vegas. She had gotten bored with L.A. There was just not enough for her to do. But Vegas, well, she sucked that energy right into her.

After her escape from her prison inside that mirror, she spent a good year underground, hiding and learning. She sucked energies from televisions and radios. She was able to learn about the world she was in and how much she could shine. At her full glory, her eyes were diamonds and gold; she would sparkle bright and nothing around could help but keep their eyes on her.

In modern day America, she could still sparkle, but the glow was minimal. She couldn't do anything about her golden eyes, and she would always have sparkles in her mass of hair as well as her skin. But in Vegas, people seemed to cover themselves in glitter and wear things on their eyes that made them all sorts of colors.

It was four in the morning, and she was on a dance floor. She had the bottom half of her gown in her arms, some Versace she had convinced someone to buy her the day before. Learning their names would be a waste of time - so many men for so many diamonds and dresses and dinners and jewels. So, to simplify things, she called them all Rich.

They didn't care, for Cassiopeia Dumont was the most attractive creature that they ever would see. Plus, with a wave of her hand, she could just vanish from their eyesight all together. As the crowd moved in, she felt a gush of wind start to form about her. Knowing what this was she began to cast in her head. She was rusty, though. She had no reasons to cast spells in the almost twenty years she had been back. An enchantress' touch is enough.

"Fuck."

Cassiopeia released her muscles and allowed herself to be engulfed by the wind. Vanishing off the dance floor, the energy in the club immediately shifted, and no one seemed to be having as much fun as they were a second ago.

Cassiopeia was in a grandiose garden, encompassed in glass that seemed to be diamond crusted. No one could see in or out. What a garden. Down a long line of steps led way into the most beautiful field she had ever seen. Tall unique trees with colors both vibrant and explosive, the ground was covered in patterns and swirls of majestical reminders of what nature could be. She knew where she was.

"Sister?" Cassiopeia called out, letting her dress fall to the floor. She felt no interference here, no cellphones or televisions. She was glowing, and sparkles were slowly falling off of her. Her power was at its strongest here.

"Sister."

Gwen was sitting at the top of the ancient stone steps Cassiopeia had just walked down. Her beauty wasn't hidden here. One could tell she was a girl of about eighteen, not this between sixteen and forty nonsense. Her hair was also down, completely, one long mane of gorgeous amber hair.

"Changing your look?" Cassiopeia smiled. "Where are we?"

"Where I'll end up." Gwen was fiddling with a final string that was particularly tied tight in the back of her hair. "I thought before this all begins we should at least see each other. I know you've been partying it up. Little different from maenads and bacchus, eh?"

"I'd rather they throw glitter than spill blood." Cassiopeia looked off at a tree that twisted about itself and ended in purple flowers that were slowly dripping dew. "Why haven't you reached out to me? I've been back now..."

"About twenty years. We barely have a place on this earth, but you seemed to be enjoying yourself. I didn't want to ruin your fun by bringing you here."

Cassiopeia looked back towards her sister and half smiled. Only half because if she brought her here for a warning...

"Witches have been reading prophecies now since our world broke apart. Come a few days from now you must go to the Hotel Amira in California. An archeologist uncovered an ancient box that he claims dates back further than he ever has seen before. From Egypt. He doesn't have the key for the box, but it will be on display at the Hotel. I fear his Lord Master Voodoo King…"

"Oh stop it," Cassiopeia rolled her eyes. "Can we just call him Michael? His ego is outrageous."

"His ego started a war for you. His ego then imprisoned you in a mirror because you wouldn't marry him. You've been as reckless as I'd figure you'd be. It's in your blood and nature - you can't just stay hidden. You are meant to shine. You need to be at that hotel because I need your full power. I need you to give Vegas a break and take a vacation there. But be prepared, Cassiopeia, because I can tell your muscle is weak. Maybe blast a few oceans apart, or explode rocks on top of a mountain before you go…"

"While I've been encaged… he's been practicing magic. Learning different tricks and probably building an army. You want me, alone, to face him?" Cassiopeia laughed and shook her head, massive amounts of sparkles falling down around her. "Maybe you should have taken a rest in a mirror, cause that was so much fun."

"I've been busy." Gwen flipped the string from out of her hair and put it in a bag, a bag that was full with the gems and strings and jewels. "Saving people. Hurling Michael's demons back down into their grave. Stopping Abaddon…"

"I forgot about your winged… friend." Cassiopeia giggled on the word friend. "Have you been spending…?"

"You know me better than that, sister." Gwen looked up annoyed. "He's in a cage."

"A cage!?" Cassiopeia went up the stairs and sat next to her sister. As their arms brushed, a surge of energy passed through them, almost as if they just caught up with each other. "Oh… I honestly forgot…"

"We have that type of bond?" Gwen smiled at her sister. "I won't be at the fight with you, sister. But I will be…"

"… setting him free." Cassiopeia put her head on Gwen's shoulder for a second. "I miss the days where all we had to worry about was…"

"Just being alive." Gwen smiled, and a small tear formed at her eye that she quickly wiped away. "These people… They don't appreciate nature and beauty like we did. If they don't have their phones on them it's like it never happened. No one looks up anymore. They are all marching this march with their heads down. But… when Vega rises… stand on the side of good."

"I will."

"Vega will see how this world works. Money. Smartphones. Stocks. Materialism. Nothing will stop her disapproval. Last time she broke the world in two. This time she could end it forever. Goodbye sister."

"Goodbye Gwen."

A gust of powerful wind and Cassiopeia was back on the dance floor. The club immediately began to pick up momentum. The energy in the room was brighter than ever, and people immediately began to join the line outside.

As Cassiopeia danced, she twisted her hands towards the sky bouncing energy to and from the stars, and let a single tear fall from her eye. Then they streamed, beautiful tears of diamonds and gold.

That would be the last time she would see her sister.

Julia sat on her porch. One of her kittens was licking her ear, the small black one with huge green eyes. Julia hated to have a favorite, but Mystery was just that. At five years old, she really was now a cat, but she never grew. One morning when Julia came to the shelter, she found Mystery scratching at the front door. She never left her side and had caught a bee from stinging Julia once. Yup, Mystery was her favorite.

Julia sat on her porch. The autumn leaves had begun to fall, and down the road some kids were toilet papering the house of a teacher. Goosey night. It was something Julia had participated in many times as a kid, a night where you are technically allowed to cause mischief. Why not? Plus, she had friends in high school who liked to push the limits of fun.

Julia sat on her porch.

Hecate appeared in a blue flame. Her eyes were surprised that Julia was sitting there. Julia could feel her power from across the lawn. On the totem pole of witchcraft, Hecate was but a maggot.

Hecate shook her head and got a mean look in her eye. Julia wondered what string she pulled from the inside for that to happen. As she began to approach her, Julia stood and flexed her muscle.

"Enough." Julia commanded at Hecate, and the word hit Hecate alone setting her in place. "You are not welcome in my home."

"I'm here on a peace mission."

"You are here to kill my husband and then make sure I stand with you at the world's end." The kitten was on her shoulder nuzzling her neck as to comfort her. "You are not getting a step closer."

"I can kill your kitten." Hecate shot her hand up, but Julia raised hers. The fireball that twisted out of Hecate's fingers fell to ashes before even approaching her. "You are in your thirties, and I am older than I even remember. You can't overpower me! Not even with your aunt's powers in you!"

"Wrap her up." Julia raised her hand and out of the grounds vines began to circle around Hecate. "Where is he?"

"Who? Ouch, stop it! Ugh! What's with you and your aunt and vines with long thorns!" The vines began to tighten around Hecate and wrap and wrap and wrap and... "He'll kill me if I tell you where he is! He'll tear me shred by shred!"

"That wasn't the right answer. When you go back to your master, tell him I will not stand with you and that I will stand with the others who are against this. I have a feeling we are outnumbering you at this point, so wouldn't it make more sense to join us instead of failing over and over again? That must make you so mad."

"Watch your tongue little one. He'll eat your heart for dinner."

"Wrong answer." Julia grasped her fist together, and the vessel in which Hecate inhabited burst open. The skin fell, and strings upon strings upon strings fell with it. From inside, the spinning wheel grew to its actual size, and so did Hecate who immediately tossed her cloak over her head. Hecate was an old hag, and though Julia didn't see her face, she saw her hand, which was weakly pointing up towards her.

"Wrong move little witch." Hecate coughed into her sleeves and vanished the spinning wheel into her cloak. "When we meet again, it won't be this easy. When we meet again…"

"I'll see you at the Hotel Amira," Julia said standing her ground, twisting her hands allowing the vines to wrap back to the ground.

Hecate waited as if to be transported away, but nothing. She let out an enraged sound. In a bustle of dusty cloaks, she made her way down the street as quickly as she could, for without a vessel she could be killed, though Julia felt no threat from her on this night.

The kitten bit at her ear lobe slightly.

"No, Mystery." Julia side eyed her kitten. "No death tonight."

But Julia was sure, there was plenty of death to come.

Julia had already purchased rooms at the Hotel Amira on the weekend of the coming. She told Aiden she needed a spa retreat.

When this is over, Julia thought, *I will go back to my normal life. I will go back to how things were.*

The kitten nuzzled deeper into her neck, as if to comfort her, from the lie she just told herself in her head.

Sera was at the front desk at the Hotel Amira, her head hurting ever since the night before. She was still trying to comprehend what was happening to her and around her. She was so lost in thought that she missed the woman standing there.

"Checking in."

"Yes, of course. Welcome to the Amira Hotel. Can I offer you some champagne?"

"Of course, thank you." The woman with blue lips smiled as she opened her small jeweled purse to remove her credit card. "Such a nice welcome to such a beautiful hotel."

Sera ran the card and handed it back looking at the reservation.

"Mia, it seems like you are here with us for two weeks." Sera looked up and was taken aback. Mia was stunning with dark hair, light blue eyes, pale skin, and dark blue lips. Sera had never seen a woman like her before. "You requested a grand suite on our highest floor and extra fans put in the room. Our hotel has AC, and we've never…"

"Be a dear and humor me," Mia smiled. "I tend to get warm even when the AC is on full blast. Also, I requested each day a bath full of ice. A beauty regiment only some can handle… You have a pleasant glow to you. Your name?"

"Sera."

"Short for Serafina?"

"Yes. Not many people could guess that."

Mia just smiled and didn't respond. Taking her glass of champagne, she gave Sera a look over, a look of approval, and began making her way towards the elevator. Three bellboys were needed with rolling carts to get all of her bags upstairs.

"Ouch." Sera's head was killing her. "This migraine."

"My little petunia has a migraine?!" the overly exaggerated voice of her boss came from behind her. "Go home. Go rest. You don't take vacation days, and it's impossible to get you to take breaks…"

"I'm fine, really."

"No! I will not hear of it. You said you had a headache. So go. Go home!"

"Fine." Sera and her boss exchanged smiles. He had actually won this round. So she liked to work - sue her. Ryan worked at a surf job part time, which was okay at twenty, and spent all day smoking weed and playing Call of Duty.

Sera guessed surprising him wouldn't be the end of the world.

She sat in her loaner car, a jump from her normal Volkswagen beetle that everyone said fit her fun personality. She opened the book.

Chapter 2
Are You a Good Witch or Are You a Bad Witch?

Nothing else. A witch? Right. A magic book with disappearing ink or some illusion trick. She hadn't committed to taking this thing seriously yet. How it knew her name or that a maid was coming at that exact time? Sera couldn't explain it, nor could she explain what happened the night before with her car.

As she drove home, she just missed the yellow light to the turn for her apartment complex. Witch. Ok then.

If I am a witch, have the light turn green. Sera thought. *NOW!*

An explosion rattled her headache as the traffic light exploded. All of the other lights turned red, but until they replaced it, the light she wished would be green was forever 'go.' Sera laughed to herself and then desperately wished for someone to talk to. Feeling like therapy might be a good idea at this point...

Ryan would listen. He had been the best thing that had happened to her over the past few years. Working long hours like she did, coming home to his warm chest and big arms was her glass of wine at the end of the day. Together they would figure out what this book was and what was going on with Sera.

She parked the loaner car down the way as someone was in her spot. She grabbed the backpack out of the car and with haste made her way to the stairs. For some reason, she felt like if she took the elevator that might explode as well.

Sera made her way down the hallway of her chic apartment building. It had only been finished a few years ago. It wasn't cheap, and at her age, being able to afford such a place just nodded to how good of a worker she was.

As she neared her apartment door, she smelled the pot smoke. She told him time and time again to just smoke outside. The only time they smoked together was in bed. Otherwise, stepping outside killed no one. Legal or not, some people just don't like the smell, and it's courteous to others.

Sera opened the door, and music was blasting from their bedroom. Ryan had a pull-up bar in their closet and tended to like to do body workouts in there when he wasn't surfing. Sera placed her backpack down and closed the door behind her.

"Ryan, let's spend the afternoon having sex and smoking weed." Sera needed some TLC. "But first I need to talk…"

As she approached the bedroom door, it wasn't her hand that opened it but her mind. In the midst of riding him was the blonde from the night before, the one who ran out of the building when Sera came home early. Ryan had a look on his face that Sera had been certain was just for her. They were deep into it, her breasts in his face and his hands scratching down her back. Sera stood there and began to shake.

The blonde turned her head and fear was in her eyes.

"Ryan…"

Ryan looked up from the blonde's gigantic fake breasts, saw Sera, and went to get up. Sera clinched her fist, and the sheets began to tie themselves around the two lovers like handcuffs. Ryan went to speak. Sera waved a hand, and part of the sheet wrapped his mouth silencing him.

"Are you a good witch or are you a bad witch?" Sera let out in a raspy voice as she clinched her fist harder. The windows of the apartment building exploded one by one. Each felt like a relief inside of her. But then the energy was swirling in and around her. She was sucking it in, the power, the force, the ultimate gift or curse. Sera looked over at the iPod dock and mentally raised the music to its maximum level, one that would drown out screams.

"Bad."

The door to the bedroom slowly began to close.

No one would be able to hear the terror cries of screams.

In the middle of Alabama, in the middle of a dense forest that you almost cannot get through, in a clearing, stands an old building. At one point, it was a steel mill, but that was back in the 1800s. At one point, roads led here, and it was bustling building America's first railroads. But now, no one got near it. It sat in ruins, and even *Ghostfaces* was going to do a special there but quickly decided against it. The energy radiating from it was so strong - the only thing that got near it was crows. Lots and lots of crows. They sang night and day, a melancholy song, a song you'd hear at a graveyard or funeral.

Gwen was in the basement of the gigantic building, rubbing her nail across a board. She picked up enough dust to make a fist size ball. Her long amber hair was down and beautiful, fresh and healthy, and her jade gown was spinning about her. Her glamour spell was un-cast and she looked eighteen, the age she was when Vega broke the world apart.

"Etse ne end ets ne ense." She held her hand up at the wall, and it began to shake, the wooden panels cracking at their edges, slowly disintegrating. "Abaddon sayne fezee Abaddon sole merlaceay!"

The wood panels exploded off, and Gwen covered herself as a tidal wave of dust exploded out with it. She coughed as the dust fell, and all that was in front of her now were bars. It was a jail she had created a few hundred years back with bars of red and crimson substances that floated in place.

"Gwen..." A deep luscious voice rose from the darkness, filled with hope. "I would know your voice anywhere."

"Abaddon."

"Why… no… not why, why's and here's and there's. They don't matter." Two large hands grasped at the red bars that enclosed Abaddon in darkness. Slowly a face came into view, a perfectly chiseled face, with ivory skin like a statue, a strong bone structure, and plump lips. His eyes were feminine and huge, blue and sad, and his eye lashes were long. Locks of dark hair fell around his face and right above his shoulders. "You have come for me?"

"In a way," Gwen sniffled and straightened herself. "It felt like yesterday I put you here."

"Not for me." Abaddon turned and walked back into his cell of darkness. It was large enough so he could pace; Gwen had made sure of that. "I have begun feeling time, seconds, minutes, and hours. You put me here for hundreds of years, and I've been counting the days, feeling the sun rise and fall. You knew it was me who freed your mind from that horrid serial killer - you know we have that type of connection. I destroyed him and sent him to nowhere. I set you free and still… you didn't come see me."

"You…" Gwen shook herself and the tear at her eye away. "You had turned this place into a breeding ground. Putting your seed in a hundred women. People still tell the story these days of me giving birth to a child with hoofs and horns. They, for some reason, didn't know the whole story - which I would never tell them. You had kidnapped at least a hundred women. You forced yourself upon them…"

"You never asked me why. I love you."

"I didn't need to know why!" Gwen turned away, and the memories of the past made her fist squeeze. "Hecate was here helping you birth these things. You took on a witch so dumb she wound up in a Shakespeare book. You can't kidnap people, and you can't rape people. The why…"

"You are barren. All the women of your line are. You are Mother Nature, not meant to be a mother." Abaddon interrupted her, and his eyes were just visible from his cell. Soft blue eyes, caring eyes, eyes filled with so much pain and yearning. "I wanted us to have a family. We could have been together. Put all of the other stuff behind us and raised these children like our own. Don't you miss my wings around you? Don't you miss the electricity when we…"

"They had hoofs and horns!" Gwen roared at him. In a sound of wings flapping, Abaddon retracted to the back of his cell. "You don't grasp the concept of love. Of family. Of this world. This isn't ancient Rome or Greece or Egypt or Africa. These are civilizations that do not worship us - who were we to be worshipped in the first place? So we survived a sonic boom from the most powerful of our kind. She's returning Abaddon."

"Impossible," he said with arrogance in his voice as he shuffled in darkness. "She's buried so deep and under so many spells…"

"That are being undone. You don't get it. The technology these humans have, the libraries of knowledge they are connected to. They found the box, somewhere deep in Egypt. Rapture is coming, Abaddon. I need you to be there. I need you to not bow to her and accept a crown of terror. I need you to fight. I need your wings to turn white again."

Silence spread, the echoes of their conversation vanishing into the walls of the ancient building. The only sound was the murder of crows squawking above.

"Nevermore," Gwen whispered. "Nevermore."

"What?"

"Promise yourself to me."

"Forever, my love. Forever and ever. I will do right by you. I love one. I love only. I love you."

Gwen raised her hand towards the cage, and the bars fell. Inside you could hear a stretching sound, and then the cracking of strange bones after sockets that hadn't been stretched in hundreds of years.

A grand flutter of wings.

"I love you, fool."

Gwen looked at her hand and blew at it. It burst into flames as a hungry fire enwrapped her entire body turning her to dust.

"NO!"

It was a sound that rang throughout the building and through the skies. The small town adjacent swore they had heard it. The crows began to sing louder and more incessantly. In the darkness, Abaddon closed his hand, and every crow began to fall, a hundred or more, instantly dead falling to the ground.

He opened his hand, and they all popped back to life and flew away never to return to the building. In a burst of energy, the building exploded outwards creating a perfect circle. The townsfolk claimed they saw a creature flying into the sky. Some said it was Superman. Others said it was a dark angel with wings that expanded yards. A nun claimed it was a sign from God, and He had sent an angel for an upcoming battle - she had been the closest with her claim.

They could all agree on one thing though: he was heading west... towards California.

Goodbye

My name is Thomas Jabniel Featherstone.

I am one of the only members of the Featherstone family remaining. Over the past few months, men in my family have been slain all over the country. It has been the ways that they have been dying. It feels like someone has been reading the plot line to *The Conjuring* or *Insidious* to me. Dark murky figures, lights flickering, giant scratch marks along the walls, rocking chairs... all around 3am. Then, an uncle gone, a cousin gone, a great uncle missing...

Cassiopeia spoke to me through a mirror for most of my early childhood. She told me of a world before our own, one we know as Pangea. One they had no name for, for it was just their world, their kingdom. She told me of the darkness of the night. She warned me of the coming monsters.

Who only takes demonology courses in college? This guy. It helped me enough to stop a few of these dark creatures, making many mistakes along the way. I set fire to a woman who I thought was a witch, but it was her daughter. She then tossed water on her mother, and then there was an electrical fire...

Every instrument needs a fine tune. Every new player needs practice.

Praise Gwen.

Gwen had passed information onto my mind… much more than Cassiopeia ever did… Upon this kingdom from where she came was a place where it was normal for 'people' to have wings, powers, abilities and tricks up their sleeves. In this land… only a few stood out. More powers than the others, more abilities than the rest, a few who could not only fly but raise the dead, or not only shine but seduce and throw rays of sun. This was a magical place… until one night when dark clouds festered the skies and lightning struck the earth and so rose beasts, demons, and blood thirsty beings.

Also with them, a dark queen.

Vega rose from a fire that could not be put out.

Not as a baby, not as a child, but a creature of utter beauty that radiated power. Without having to move a hand, she would shift the grounds… and she did. Angered with the way 'her' kingdom was run, she clapped her hands and all was done. The ground below broke and spread. The beginning of continents, the beginning… the beginning…

Dearest Grandmother, how much you knew about this, or if we play a part in this, I'll never know. I had so many questions to ask you before you passed. But, with all the knowledge Gwen has passed and the journey I'm set on…

Questions shall be answered.

As an ancient witch once said…

"By the pricking of my thumb…
        Something Wicked this Way Come." (Second
Witch. 1611 - Hecate needs to stop claiming that line.)

        But so will I.

                This is not goodbye.

This is an end of tales, of battles, of grasps at clues and
understanding.

We shall all meet again at the Hotel Amira in California.

ABOUT THE AUTHOR

Christian Jeremy Alecci resides in Bergen County, NJ. Christian splits his time between health and nutrition in the role of a certified personal trainer. In his free time he pursues his love and passion of writing, CEO of CFPublishing. He enjoys all things macabre, and finds inspiration from his favorite author Stephen King as well as high fantasy novels. Also is the author of Avon Hush and Suburbia.

Fun Fact: CJ thinks he would be the first victim in the horror movie. Hopefully his writing is better than his chance of survival.

www.ingramcontent.com/pod-product-compliance
Lightning Source LLC
Chambersburg PA
CBHW020555180626
46810CB00007B/2521